To Let Love Prosper

AR TEDESCHI

Indovinello Vento Books, LLC

This is a work of fiction. Any resemblance to actual people, living or dead, or existing businesses and churches, is coincidental. Geographical locations are noted, with some being fictitious and other in the common domain. The Pryor Mountain Wild Horse Range is an actual protected refuge in the state of Montana for free roaming mustang horses. The National Football League team, Seattle Seahawks, is mentioned, along with several actual universities, including the United States Military Academy West Point; however, any discussion of their programs and protocols is fictitious.

Published by Indovinello Vento Books, LLC

ISBN: 978-1-7348476-1-1
Library of Congress Control Number: 2024925180

Cover art by David Munoz
www.davidmunozart.com

Table of Contents

1. *Arrival*

Katelyn bounded down the wide staircase, whispering frantically to herself, "Please – let me not be late. Let me not be late." She swung around the large second-floor landing, gripping the heavy wooden banister as she flew down the remaining steps. She barely glanced out the huge picture window framing the landing, focused on reaching the crowd already gathered below in the large dining hall of the ranch.

As she skipped the last step and leapt to the floor she sighed with relief. The person attempting to corral the 40 young adults was not the ranch foreman. She hurried, her heart still pounding, toward a mass of curly brown hair towering above the sea of heads. She wormed her way through the jostling crowd to a tall, muscular man. Linking her arm in his, she looked up and smiled. The top of her shining raven hair, pulled back in a ponytail, just reached to his chin.

"Good morning, Ben" she said catching her breath, her bright aquamarine eyes sparkling with excitement.

Ben looked down at Katelyn with a surprised smile. "Good timing," he said. "You and Natalie missed breakfast, but looks like you will be in time to hear Josiah sermonize the day before we start working. Where is Nat?" he asked, glancing around.

"She told me to go down without her. You know mornings aren't really her thing."

"Yeah, but breakfast is. You listen to Josiah, while I go make her a plate before they clean up everything. You want anything?"

Katelyn shook her head at Ben's kind gesture and reluctantly let go of his arm. "I'm fine," she said, watching the group of college students briefly part like goslings making way for the head goose as Ben made his way to the food counter.

Her attention was drawn back to the front of the group as a young man, his slender frame dressed in a red flannel shirt over crisp denim jeans, stood on a bench seat and tried to quiet the talkative and energetic crowd. The clamor continued until he just shouted with a grin, "Hey, listen up everybody!"

"Good," he said as the group quieted to a dull murmuring and whispers. "We have an opportunity to be both Martha and Mary today at Singing Stream."

Katelyn shook her head with a frustrated breath at how Josiah could always find a way to turn an opportunity into a sermon. The grimaces around her looked like her friends had similar thoughts. The young people were a smaller crowd from the very large college and career group at the Spokane, Washington mega-church, "Abundant Life," and had arrived late last night. Josiah was the group's pastor.

Their outreach program included helping local businesses with major projects. Singing Stream Horse Ranch, located in the heart of Montana near the Wyoming border, was far from their usual volunteer spots. However, it provided a unique opportunity to help the ranch prepare for winter while also offering an ideal location for a fall retreat. Room and board were a fair trade for helping around the ranch in the middle of the beautiful southern Montana hills.

Katelyn grew more exasperated as Josiah kept talking, wondering why he couldn't feel the young people's energy to start exploring and working at the ranch, not listen to a Bible teaching. Her attention wandering, she glanced around the room, seeing the large dining hall for the first time in daylight. The room was framed by large wooden logs, beginning to shine as the golden morning light streaked through tall, curtained windows. The exposed roof and its heavy wooden beams rose over 40 feet above the rough polished plank floor, with a massive oak staircase leading to the two upper levels of dormitory rooms. Photographs of horses lined the walls, along with what looked like original watercolor paintings of the surrounding countryside. Missing were typical ranch paraphernalia, like horseshoes or spurs, or old cowboy prints. Instead, the decorations, overhead chandeliers, and flowers in scattered vases revealed a woman's touch, making the large eating space more than just a functional cafeteria. This is someone's home, she mused.

The sound of metal trays clanging and pots and pans being cleaned vibrated from the open space above the wide kitchen serving counter. Katelyn's stomach grumbled a little over the lingering smells of breakfast eggs, fried potatoes, bacon, and cinnamon coffee cake. She longingly gazed towards a second wide counter near the kitchen area containing several massive urns and pitchers, along with a soda dispensing station. "Coffee!" she whispered out loud.

She caught the eye of her father, standing near the coffee urns, who nodded with a smile. Of course, this is where he would be. He was talking to several of the other adult advisors who had volunteered to come on the retreat, but raised his eyebrows to her without stopping his conversation. She recognized that look — pay attention.

Katelyn reluctantly turned back to Josiah, who fortunately had finished and was introducing the ranch manager. Her excitement at working with horses edged up a notch as a petite young woman, who looked just a little older than herself, stepped up on the bench seat. The woman wore almost a similar flannel shirt and jeans as Josiah, but this woman appeared to be a natural ranch worker. She sported a small cowboy hat strung behind her back off a beaded leather drawstring, which laid over her long braided blond hair. Katelyn knew much about the ranch's work with wild mustangs, having researched this location for the planning committee, but was not aware of the management team.

"Hello, and welcome to Singing Stream Ranch," she opened with a joyful voice. "As Josiah mentioned, my name is Janet Ingersoll, and I will be coordinating your activities and assigning tasks during your stay here."

Janet's poise and ease with the large crowd was inspiring for someone so near Katelyn's age. I have got to talk with her, Katelyn vowed. Ben eased back up to Katelyn as the young ranch manager began speaking. He handed her a piece of bacon in a napkin, with a cup of coffee. She thanked Ben with a grateful expression, moving her head around the tall people in front of her to catch a better view of the woman.

"Besides being the general foreman of the ranch, I am also the owner's daughter, so I say with real gratitude that we here at the ranch are very excited and grateful for your visit. I hope your time here will be just as wonderful for you as we expect from your service. Please feel free to take advantage of all the amenities, and we will be scheduling some horse riding during your weekend stay, for any who are interested."

Katelyn took in a deep breath at the mention of horses, and a slight smile inched up her face. Ben was watching her with an amused turn of his face. She felt Ben's gaze and looked up, but he had already turned back to listen to Janet.

Disappointment washed over Katelyn's face. Missing the connection with Ben immediately drew up a melancholy, like an old, musty blanket. As her joy dampened, the sounds of Janet's voice dulled into muffled echoes while the bright golden sunshine streaming into the room seemed to fade into a grey light. She had hoped to talk Ben into working with her in the stables this morning, her earlier conversations on the trip up to the ranch being unsuccessful. I'm such a hopeless failure, she thought.

Katelyn was wrenched back into the present by Ben's elbow, and she caught Janet mentioning tasks in the stable, spreading some new artificial bedding hay. Panicked that she may have missed her opportunity to work with the horses, Katelyn immediately stretched as high as she could and interrupted Janet.

"I'll take the stables!" she said with a waving hand. "My name is Katelyn."

2. Assignments

Katelyn saw Janet nod with a smile, but then noticed several of her college friends, still chuckling from her interruption, wrinkle their noses and casually step back. Even Benjamin sidestepped with an exaggerated grimace.

Katelyn looked around at her friends and settled an annoyed glance at Ben. "Well - what did you think we would be doing at a ranch?"

Ben looked at the ceiling and answered, "Brushing down sweating animals. Mucking out stalls of wet hay, and you-know-what. Gross. Sounds like why I came to a retreat in the mountains."

Janet appeared to ignore the lighthearted banter, focused on reading a list of chores from her iPad while jotting down the names of volunteers. Fence mending, changing tractor oil, fixing stuck gates, and a myriad of other tasks around the ranch were quickly divided among the young adults and their church group advisors.

As the final chores were assigned, Katelyn realized that nobody else had volunteered to help her work in the stables. She turned to Ben and punched him in the arm with more than just a playful tease. "Thanks for the support," she said.

"Hey - watch the throwing arm," he groaned with fake pain. "Final championship game in two weeks."

"Yeah sure - don't hurt yourself with all that painting you volunteered for," Katelyn said.

"Oh, don't worry," Ben responded with a wink. "Chet and Brian volunteered with me, and I'll just supervise as they do all the work. You just make sure you take a long shower after playing in the barn."

Katelyn buried her feelings at Ben, seemingly oblivious to the irritation in her voice, and watched Ben and his buddies push and shove each other out of the dining room towards the maintenance garage. Their clowning helped Katelyn retrieve a wry grin. The remaining young people and adults wandered out to their various tasks as Janet folded up her iPad. Katelyn was about to head up to her room and get her coat when Natalie, Katelyn's best friend, sidled up to her.

"You don't want to help me with the horses, Nat?" Katelyn asked in feigned surprise.

"Seriously?" Natalie replied. She threw her head to the side, imitating a shocked debutante, amusing Katelyn since Natalie's brown shimmering hair was cut in a short bob. Natalie repeated Ben's grimace.

"Sorry. This is one time when the Kat and Nat team part ways. I got myself a fun inside job of cleaning and sewing up some leather gear. I'm going to see if I can sneak some tassels on the men's saddles and sweeten up the smell of the leather with my special perfume," she laughed.

Katelyn sniffed the air around Natalie's head. "New shampoo formula?" she asked. "It smells different from anything you have concocted over the years."

"You like it?" Natalie beamed. "I tried it the first time this morning. Don't tell anyone, but I got a special shipment of some frankincense and myrrh essential oils," she whispered. "If Josiah hears about it, he will turn it into a sermon, and my whole marketing plan will go out the window. I'm going to see if it turns any of the cowboys' heads."

"Well, go on then," Katelyn said. "Me – I'm looking forward to a quiet morning just fellowshipping with the horses."

"I did hear that someone else was helping in the stables but couldn't see who might have volunteered with all the tall people jostling around," Natalie said. "I feel like I'm back in high school around some of these guys. At least the ranch manager, Janet, is our size. By the way, everything Ok with you and Ben? I did notice that your love-tap had a little more energy than normal."

"Everything's fine, Nat."

Katelyn and Natalie exchanged glances and repeated in unison, "Fine, just fine." They both smiled.

"By the way, Nat, Ben made you a plate. I think it is over at the end of the counter."

Natalie lit up at the mention of breakfast. She gave Katelyn one last flip of her imaginary long hair and said, "Have fun with the horses." She skipped over to the counter, grabbed a paper plate covered over with a mound of food, and covered it with another paper plate. She laughed back to Katelyn while holding up the plate, and skipped out of the room.

Katelyn's mood returned to her initial excitement as her friend danced off. She then ran up the massive stairs to the third-floor girls' rooms, a grin widening on her face from thinking of the horses. She dashed into the room she shared with Natalie, grabbed her winter jacket lying on the single large king-size bed, and darted back down the stairs, skipping the last several steps and leaping to the floor. She headed over to the smorgasbord counter, becoming leaner as the kitchen workers cleaned up breakfast, pocketed a couple of apples, and rushed over to Janet.

Katelyn saw Janet's amused look from watching her scurrying, but it didn't faze her. Flushed cheeks and a broad smile reflected Katelyn's anticipation.

"You pronounce your name with a long 'A,' like Kay, right?" Janet asked as Katelyn stopped in front of her. "I just heard one of your friends call you Kat."

"Yes. You probably heard my nickname from my best friend, Natalie. We have been like sisters, growing up together, inseparable. Our birthdays are almost on the same day – we celebrated our twenty-first birthdays last month. The 'Kat and Nat' phrase caught on long ago."

"Well, Katelyn with a long 'A' – let's get going," Janet smiled. "Lots of work to do, and you look eager to begin."

Katelyn followed Janet as they wandered out of the back of the dining hall into a large "mud room." It contained painted wooden benches lining the walls, scratched with years of wear and lots of dirty boots strewn about underneath them. Dozens of worn denim and leather work jackets hung around the room on metal pegs.

"Here, pick some over-boots that fit, and you might want to trade your nice ski jacket for a work coat," Janet pointed around the room. She hid a slight grin behind her hand, but the grin turned to surprise as she watched Katelyn try on several pairs of mud-spattered boots without hesitation, and lace them up without checking for scratched nail polish.

Katelyn hung up her designer ski jacket alongside several of her fellow college students' coats already on hooks and moved smoothly around the room checking for coats that had a perfect fit for her athletic build, ignoring their dried dust and smell of farm animals.

"You remind me of a good friend I had back in college," Janet said.

"How so?"

"When I first met her, I thought she belonged in a specialty shop selling perfume or modeling designer gowns on a runway, not in college. She often surprised me with her willingness to get down in the dirt."

Katelyn was a little embarrassed but simply replied, "Dirt?"

"She was a fellow veterinarian student."

Katelyn's ears perked up at the mention of vet school, though she sensed a hint of sadness in Janet's last words. Instead of probing further Katelyn buttoned up her work coat, selected a pair of used leather gloves in a bin, and pronounced, "Ready!" She noticed that Janet's earlier amusement had shifted to quiet approval.

"Is there someone else helping?" she asked as they headed out into the crisp November air.

"Yes – Ethan," answered Janet. "I talked to him earlier. He said he would meet us in the stables."

"Oh, alright."

Janet glanced at Katelyn as she closed the door. "I sense some hesitation. Will working with him be a problem? I have some other tasks that you can do."

"No," answered Katelyn, feeling slightly self-conscious at her reaction. "I just don't really know him."

Janet nodded, seeming to accept the simple explanation, and made her way out into the main yard. Katelyn was relieved that Janet didn't push for more. She tried to pinpoint the source of her uneasiness, but it was like chasing a shadow. The joy she felt working with the wild mustangs stabled at the ranch began to fade as a sudden, unsettling thought crept in, sending a shiver through her.

Ethan – he will change everything.

3. Introductions

Janet and Katelyn headed towards the stables, their boots crunching over the gravel path. Small ice crystals rimed the walkway from the light freeze last night, while a fog appeared with every exhale.

"Does it usually get this cold so early in autumn?" Katelyn asked, tightening up her work coat.

"Fall can be surprising at times," Janet smiled back at her through a wreath of frozen breath.

"And snow?" Katelyn asked with a gleam in her eye. She was an avid downhill skier and loved the winters in the mountainous Northwest.

"We are normally protected from the huge storms that sweep across this part of lower Montana by being nestled between the Bighorn and Wolf mountains. But sometimes..."

Katelyn ignored the worried frown on Janet's face with her last statement, and instead followed her gaze to the peaks off in the far distance surrounding the valley. They were a grey line against the brilliant blue sky, while the lower Ponderosa pine forests were still clouded in morning mist.

"This is such a beautiful country," said Katelyn. "And you are so close to the wild mustang herds. Working here at the Pryor Mountain Wild Horse Range, with horses actually allowed to roam free, must be a joy."

The turn in the conversation to horses erased any further discussion about the weather and soon both of them were in an animated conversation about the mustangs in the area and caring for horses. They talked excitedly about the special programs the ranch was involved with as they stepped into the working yard surrounding the stables. By the time they walked through several fenced-in areas and entered the main horse barn they were chatting like old friends.

As they headed through the large open barn doors and started down the long central pathway, Katelyn's attention was drawn to several young auburn mustangs peering out over the lower stall doors at the other end of the stable. Her eyes lit up at the first glimpse of the princely animals. Without taking her eyes off the horses, she grabbed Janet's arm and almost began skipping through the barn towards the horses.

"I told you that you would find a kindred spirit with Katelyn," an amused voice sounded from behind them.

"Ethan," Janet laughed as she stopped and spun around.

Katelyn turned with Janet; arms still linked. At first all she could see was a large mop of unruly brown hair. As she focused upon the young man leaning with crossed arms over the first stall door, she recognized the narrow light-colored face. His pale cheeks were flushed red with exertion and he sprouted a smile that stretched between his ears.

Katelyn let go of Janet and followed her back to the first stall. Janet and Ethan's friendship was confirmed as she saw Janet lay her hand upon Ethan's arm.

"You were right," Janet said glancing back at Katelyn. "It seems we do share a love for animals."

Katelyn smiled back, tamping down her questions and uneasiness at Ethan's statement. She wondered how he knew about her interest in horses when she hardly knew anything about him. It didn't help either that every time Ethan switched his gaze back to her, his face brightened.

Janet was about to begin giving instructions about the work tasks when her iPad beeped. Eyes scrunched and her brow furrowed as she read the instant message.

"I'm sorry guys. I need to head over to the north corral. We have a situation with a newly received wild mustang and one of the stock horses. Ethan, would you mind getting Katelyn going on preparing the new test beds? I should be back in a couple of hours to check up on you."

Without waiting for an acknowledgement from Ethan, she quickly turned and began jogging out of the stable. Katelyn followed Janet's departure with worried eyes.

Speaking to Janet's quickly disappearing back she quietly said, "I hope the animals are Ok. I wonder if she needs my help?"

Katelyn was surprised to hear another voice, almost forgetting that Ethan was there.

"She will be all right. Her ranch hands are a good crew."

Katelyn turned and looked at Ethan, still leaning over the stall door, with his amused eyes focused on her face. Great. Here I am left alone with this guy, and he seems a little too friendly. She began wondering again how he knew about her animal interests since they had hardly talked after she had first met him.

Ethan had showed up in Katelyn's high school in Spokane as a senior, while she was a sophomore. That was four years ago. He had been in one of her high school classes but she didn't remember talking with him much at all. She had heard that he was in his last year at Eastern Washington University, a smaller state school compared to Washington State University, where she, Natalie, and Ben had attended for the last two years.

Though she sometimes saw him at church over the years, he had never attended their college and career group events; the huge crowds at church with multiple services always seemed to get in the way of ever striking up a conversation. This was the first retreat she had ever seen him attend.

How does he know anything about me?

As though unconcerned with Katelyn's uneasiness, Ethan just continued smiling at her with his quirky grin. He removed his right-hand glove, leaned over the half-height stable door and held out his hand towards her.

"Hi," he said. "I'm Ethan McGregor. You may not remember me from AP calculus." His broad smile stretched over his white teeth as he continued. "I remember you. You didn't let the other senior math-heads get away with hazing you as a sophomore. You even beat my scores."

Katelyn's hand reached out automatically as a kind gesture to Ethan's compliment. She glimpsed joy in Ethan's unabashed stare and dark shimmering eyes. Surprisingly, he did not shake but simply held her hand while beaming through closed lips.

A long dormant spark awoke in Katelyn, and the person who used to dazzle the judges and adversaries in the debate club rose to the surface.

Narrowing her gaze, she said, "Aren't you supposed to *shake* my hand?"

Ethan glanced down at their clasped hands and replied with a broadening smile, "Normally, but this is an opportunity too good to miss." He added with a mock southern accent, "to hold the hand of a lovely lady."

Katelyn's eyebrows arched. Gripping his hand tighter, she replied, "If I remember, you were a transfer from a school in Texas. Is this how a southern gentleman behaves?"

"Texas is technically not the South. And, a gentleman never passes up an opportunity to impress a woman." Ethan slightly squeezed back at the word, "impress."

"You're impressing me?" she responded with an increased grip, and eyes that started to laugh. "Texas is clearly below the Mason-Dixon Line, and joined the South in the Civil War."

"Obviously impressing you," he grinned back. "Texans have really only been for Texas."

It was Ethan who finally relaxed and released her hand as loud, hurried footsteps in the gravel outside the stable doors echoed into the barn. Katelyn turned her head just as Ben appeared at the stable entrance.

Katelyn could see from Ben's raised eyebrows that he had caught their quickly released hands. She watched him with a growing redness in her cheeks as he frowned at Ethan's retreating arm. He moved next to Katelyn and put his arm around her shoulder. Straightening to his full six-foot four-inch height he spoke directly to Ethan.

"Hey, I've seen you around church. Ethan, right? Looks like I interrupted something. Anything I miss?"

Katelyn looked up towards Ben, her face contorted into an "Are you for real?" look. Ben kept his arm around her and continued to stare at Ethan. Ethan, watching the silent communication between the two with his amused smile, waited a couple of seconds before replying. The silence seemed an eternity to Katelyn. She was about to give her own reply to Ben when Ethan finally spoke, causing Katelyn to look at him in shock.

"Yes. I think this is my opportunity."

4. Yearning Hearts

Ben echoed Katelyn's surprise with a crinkled forehead. But before he could ask any further questions, Ethan started talking football.

"I saw your win at the PAC-12 semi-finals last weekend against USC. Do you have eyes in the back of your head? Your stats are normally impressive but you really shined last week. You were always a step ahead of the Trojan defense. I was amazed at how you read their moves."

"Uh, Ok – thanks," Ben stammered.

Katelyn's thoughts echoed Ben's apparent confusion, after Ethan's heartfelt praise. Did I really hear him say what I thought he said?

"I mean what I said about your ability to read an opponent's thinking," Ethan continued. "I've watched you play since High School. It looks like you have a special gift. I'm sure you will be a success in whatever you put your mind to after college, but have you ever considered a career in the military? You clearly have an ability to think strategically."

Ben's face reflected amazement at Ethan's words. Again, all he could reply was, "Thanks."

Katelyn looked back up to Ben hearing the confusion in his voice. "Ben – I thought you were painting. Did you change your mind and want help with the horses?"

Ben took a deep breath, released his hold around Katelyn's shoulders, and stepped back. Looking slightly disoriented he answered, "I got the guys going, and seeing Janet leave, I thought this might be a good time to catch up."

As Ben paused, Ethan said with his cheerful smile, "I may not be very strategic myself but I can tell when I need to give people some alone time." Ethan put his rake down and began to open the stall door but Ben lifted his palm to stop him.

"I don't want to stop you working. I thought Kat was alone. This can wait till later." Looking at Katelyn he asked, "If you get some free time this afternoon, Kat, come find me over in the garage area. If not - I'll talk with you after dinner. Alright?"

"Sure," she replied, slightly puzzled by Ben's odd behavior.

Ben took both her hands in his, gave her cheek a quick kiss, and then turned to leave. His last glance went to Ethan as he stopped before heading out the door.

Ben squinted his eyes and said to Ethan, "I think you have more strategic insight than you give yourself credit for."

Ethan laughed a reply, "Well, West Point didn't think so."

"You applied to West Point?" Ben asked, incredulously.

"Ancient history," Ethan said.

Ben stared at Ethan for a few seconds, shook his head slightly, and then walked out the door. Katelyn caught his last glance at Ethan, and knew Ben was not finished with this conversation.

Ethan appeared oblivious to Ben's parting concern as he turned to Katelyn and asked, "Would you like to meet the horses that are stabled here before we start working?"

"Oh yes," she replied, her face still reflecting the confusion of Ethan's words and Ben's actions. As she turned to see the heads of several horses peering out from their stalls down the corridor, she noticeably relaxed and a smile stretched across her face.

Ethan led Katelyn to the far end of the stables, where several wild mustangs were temporarily housed alongside some workhorses not in use by the ranch hands. He introduced her to the animals and watched as she quickly bonded with them, even winning over the skittish mustangs. The apples she had tucked in her pocket helped seal the friendships as she scratched their noses and showered them with gentle praise.

Katelyn spoke to the horses with words of endearment, displaying a keen knowledge of the magnificent animals. Her hands roamed over the ears and jaws as she told them how wonderful they were, examining for illnesses or injuries. She peered over the half-height stall door, and while keeping up a steady stream of communication to the animal, evaluating their legs, ankles, and hooves. She used gentle stroking motions with her hands to check their coats and manes.

"You look like you know what you are doing around these animals," Ethan said. "I really don't like riding myself. I stop at knowing which part of the horse to stay away from so I don't get kicked. Have you ridden a lot or owned any horses?"

"I have ridden some," she said as she patted down a magnificent dun-colored quarter horse. "The only animal at home is my cat. I've read a lot about horses, though."

They wandered back to the first stall Ethan had been working in where he gave her some brief instructions about spreading the new experimental bedding material in the stalls. They divided up the mucking duties and began spreading the new hay as Ethan began a steady stream of questions. Katelyn found herself easily responding to Ethan's curiosity, sharing her college plans and her time at WSU. More amazing to herself, she began expressing her passion about caring for animals. She found herself opening up to this man whose interest was clearly genuine and who knew how to listen.

They worked well as a team in each empty stall and were almost back to the horses. As they moved through the stable, they both laughed at the many horse heads peeking out into the main corridor, with cocked ears looking like they were listening intently to the discussion.

Katelyn hummed a little tune as she spread the new bedding material up against the side walls, feeling more at home in the stable than she had anywhere else in a long time. Forgotten were Ethan's strange words at his friendly questions.

I can't believe how much I've shared with Ethan, Katelyn thought. I've never opened up with anyone new this easily before. There's something about him I can't put my finger on.

She glanced up at him as he lifted the heavy bedding sacks and emptied them on the floor. He had a quiet strength about him that filled the air with a warm peace. In the stillness between her talking she realized that she hadn't asked Ethan a thing about himself. Her thoughts were interrupted by Ethan's voice again.

"Katelyn," he started, as he planted his rake in the bedding while holding the handle under his chin with both hands. The smile and joyful face he had all morning was gone. In its place was a thoughtful squint of dark brown eyes and pressed lips, like he was poised to share a secret. "I hope I haven't badgered you too much. I have admired you for a long time and getting to know you has been a real blessing. Would you mind a more personal question?"

Ethan's statement immediately raised Katelyn's uneasiness again. First the cryptic reply to Ben about an "opportunity" and now "admiring." Only his gentle look kept her discomfort from winning the battle.

She stiffly replied, "That is always a silly question that one can't answer until the statement is asked — but sure, give it a try."

"Well," he started. "I read in a sports magazine that the Seahawks may be looking at hiring Ben for next season, before he graduates. He has amazing talent, and I guess he would leap at it. Do you have any plans should he take their offer?"

Katelyn paused. Ok, this sounds safe enough. Many evenings of conversations with Ben and Natalie on this very topic flitted through her memory. It was private, but surprisingly, Katelyn found that she wanted to talk about it. Something was still unsettled in her heart about the whole matter. Maybe sharing it with Ethan would help her understand the questions in her heart.

"We have talked about it and come up with some tentative plans should the offer come through. Both Natalie and I would transfer to the University of Washington and share an apartment. She would finish her chemistry degree and I would complete my pre-law degree. The U-dub has one of the best legal programs in the country. I would catch Ben in between practices and games and help him with his online work at the U, to complete his engineering degree."

As Katelyn finished her short explanation, the pieces of their plan, though logical and practical, still floated around in her head; they didn't feel tamped down into something solid, yet. Ethan's next words threatened to scatter them to the winds.

"You seem to have a passion for working with animals. Why pre-law?" Surprise flashed across Katelyn's face followed by a variety of emotions. She took a breath and stammered a reply.

"My dad...well, my mom was always proud of my negotiating skills...my dad would be awfully disappointed if I didn't follow in his footsteps as a trial lawyer."

Katelyn turned quickly away from Ethan and slowly dragged her rake over the floor. The questions were definitely getting a little too personal. Memories surfaced. Strange chemical smells, a starched rough blanket clutched in her hands, and the sounds of medical monitors flooded her thoughts.

Katelyn kept her back to Ethan. She tried to keep her tears a secret, brushing her glove against her face as if there was only dust on her cheek. Her quick side glance towards Ethan showed him back to work. Ten points for you Ethan – you stopped asking me questions.

As her emotions settled down Katelyn heard a familiar voice enter the stable.

"Hi guys. I'm back," Janet announced.

She had two large paper sacks in one hand while her other clasped her ever-present iPad.

Neither her face nor her words indicated to Katelyn that Janet had picked up on any of the tension of her last words.

"I need to shift both of your workloads to address an issue we have with a couple of mares and with a major change in the weather that might hit us this weekend," she said.

"Ethan, would you please head over to the north feed storage lot? I asked Ben to meet you there and help with loading hay bales onto several trailers. Ben had the painters all working smoothly, so he is moving the trailers as we speak. When you're done you can head back here and finish up. Ben will deliver the trailers to the south range where our ranch hands will unload. Here are two lunches for you and Ben when you get hungry."

"Will do," Ethan replied. "Thanks for the lunch. I'm starved."

"Yeah. I expected that. There are two sandwiches for each of you. Just don't go all slow on me and want to take a nap after eating."

"I don't know. Dozing under this blue Montana sky sounds really good right now."

Katelyn caught a slight frown from Janet and Ethan's reply, and saw that Ethan had also picked up the same vibe.

"Are you thinking that I might be interrupted by a thunderstorm?" Ethan joked as he put up his tools.

"Nothing to worry about. Just watching a potential storm front southwest of here."

Ethan just nodded but Katelyn caught a concern that didn't match her words. Ethan finished hanging up his tools and started walking out of the stable. Katelyn had used the time when they were talking to compose herself. Fortunately, she hadn't put on any eye makeup this morning.

"You guys have made a great dent in spreading the new bedding," Janet said, turning to Katelyn. "How about a change? A couple our stock horses got injured in a confrontation with a mustang. The doctor is on his way. Would you like to watch? I think you will find it interesting."

"That sounds neat! I'd love to."

"Great. We'll grab some lunch on our way out."

Ethan looked back as he walked out of the barn and caught Katelyn with his eyes. "Catch you later," he smiled.

The intensity of Ethan's gaze surprised Katelyn, and she muttered softly to his retreating back, "What are you really saying?" She blushed slightly as Janet overheard her and gave her an amused look. Janet and Katelyn hung up the remaining tools and closed the stable door.

Janet said, "I have only known Ethan for about a year, but I can tell you this. He is not very good at hiding his feelings."

Katelyn buttoned up her collar to keep herself warm and hide the redness inching up her neck. One part of her wanted to have Ethan explain himself and another hoped that observing the veterinarian would take all afternoon. What drew her attention instead was why Janet kept smiling.

5. Stallions

They worked silently, throwing the large hay bales on the trailers. Hook, lift, and stack. Ben enjoyed the simple activity; no competition – just a team working on a common goal. He smiled to himself, while noticing Ethan seemed to be in his own world, listening to music with a peculiar grin.

After loading the first trailer, they climbed into the back for a lunch break. Their breath hung in the cold air like twin exhaust plumes as they leaned against the hay bales, devouring their sandwiches, fruit, and soda.

Their time together thus far had been nearly silent, with only the grunts of exertion and sighs from a filling lunch. Ben glanced over at Ethan as he wiped his mouth and could see that Ethan's grin was a little wider. As Ethan tucked his ear buds into his pocket, Ben felt it was time for serious discussion.

"So – Ethan. Katelyn. Let's talk."

"Alright," Ethan answered. "As long as you share, too."

"Really?" Ben said. "About what?"

"West Point."

Ben stared at Ethan with a growl. What about the academy? Was he trying to avoid his earlier strange words about an "opportunity?" This was not starting out well at all.

"Sure. You go first," he said, trying to stay out front of whatever Ethan was going to reveal.

Both men shifted their seats on the hay bales to look across the trailer at each other. Ethan picked up a piece of straw, started chewing on it, and leaned back.

"How about West Point, first?" Ethan said. Without waiting for a response from Ben, Ethan kept speaking.

"My father graduated from there and was always sharing tales of his great experiences."

Against his desire to steer this conversation towards Katelyn, Ben's eyebrows raised. Ethan continued.

"We visited several times while he was on leave, and that watered the seeds he had planted while I was a little child. Have you ever visited the Academy?" he abruptly shifted a question to Ben.

Ben shook his head. "Not yet," he said. Ben tried to keep a straight face but felt like Ethan was seeing right through him.

"I remember my awe of the cadets marching on parade," Ethan continued. "I was dazzled by the cool wooded grounds and the view overlooking the Hudson River. Once, I was sitting on a bench on the parade grounds, next to the ancient cannons aimed out over the river, and an officer came up and sat by me. He shared some history of the Academy's earliest days as a fort and its importance to the young nation. I don't remember much but I can still feel his pride in serving our country. I was hooked."

"But here you are?" Ben asked. His curiosity aroused, he prodded Ethan, "I understand you are about to graduate from Eastern. What happened?"

Ethan's face flashed a small bit of sadness. He looked to the distant peaks but Ben could see that Ethan was focused on something else.

"Maybe a little more background to answer your question. My father died in Operation Desert Storm. A road mine took out his command car and he was severely injured. Then the firefight started. We got back his body, a flag, and several medals."

Ben drooped a little onto the hay bale.

"My mom somehow couldn't take the stress and she died, too, several days after his memorial service." I got shuffled around as a teenager to various relatives, and finally landed with my Aunt Desirée, my mom's sister in Texas."

Forgotten in Ben's mind was the strange outburst of an opportunity about Katelyn. His lips moved silently, struggling to find some words. He made a small grimace that accompanied feelings he hadn't considered for a long time. Ethan paused and continued to gaze beyond the hills.

"Wow - sorry," Ben said. "I can't begin to say I understand what you went through, Ethan, but I can relate a little." Ben stopped, his eyes mirroring Ethan's focus on the past. He had not shared with anyone in a long time about his own history, and he hoped the remark would fly over Ethan's head.

Ethan instead pounced on it. "Really? How can you relate?"

Ben hesitated, then said, "I was adopted."

"Tragedy?" Ethan finally asked after several quiet moments.

"Nothing so difficult as what you went through. I was adopted almost as an infant to some great parents. When I turned thirteen, my parents shared the truth. It really didn't mean much since they were the only family I have ever known, but afterwards." Ben paused, and tried to center his thoughts.

Ethan picked up another piece of straw but kept still.

Ben searched for a way to turn the conversation around and off of the emotions surfacing in his heart.

"Man, it must have been brutal in the hot Texas sun with such pale skin," Ben finally said to break the tension. As he said it Ben was immediately disgusted at such a stupid line.

"Trying to 'lighten' the conversation, Ben?" Ethan smiled back. Ben scrunched his face at the bad pun, but Ethan's casual words and humor eased the strain. Against his early inclinations, Ben started to respect this strange man.

"Your fair-skin question is actually not far from the truth," Ethan continued, as if Ben had never shared about being adopted. "When Aunt Desirée and I decided to move, we set our sights on the north, where we would not have to buy cases of sunscreen. But the main reason for our move was to improve my odds of getting into the Academy. Too much competition in Texas. So, my aunt found a job up here in cloudy Spokane at Sacred Heart Hospital - a new start for both of us. I got an additional nomination through Senator Javiss, along with a presidential nomination because my dad was in the service. Everything looked like it was a slam dunk until I got results back from my entry physical."

Ben squinted his eyes and cocked his head in an unspoken question. He subconsciously flexed his muscles knowing the difficult physical tests required for Academy acceptance, but Ethan's wiry frame and the way he handled the hay bales suggested a strong and powerful body.

"Oh, I easily passed the physical and endurance exams," Ethan replied to Ben's questioning look. "It was not that I wasn't strong enough. Do you know that the military now does extensive genetic testing?" he asked Ben, looking straight into his eyes.

"I heard something about that," Ben said, trying not to show any emotion.

Ethan smiled at Ben's answer.

"They now want some very positive genetic markers, and don't want some others. I had the bad ones. My aunt did the research on their cryptic rejection letter and found that I have a gene that messes with my heart under heavy physical and mental pressure. It's part of the same DNA that causes my skin to be so pale. I was too much of a risk for the Army."

Ben struggled with his growing empathy, but his emotions triggered his strategic mind. He considered that Ethan's mom may have had the same genetic issue, causing her untimely passing.

Ethan continued, apparently ignoring Ben's musings. "But a lot of good things are working out now that I never could have imagined. Stuff that would never have happened if I had gone to the Academy."

Ben thought that the conversation was finally getting back to Katelyn, which was fine – this was all getting much too personal. While he sensed that Ethan had left out some key parts of his story, he felt a strange kinship with this man.

"You got a nomination from a senator, Ethan," Ben said. "You succeeded academically and physically over hundreds of applicants and made it all the way through the grueling physical exams. That's something to be really proud of."

"Thanks. You sound like you are well acquainted with the process. Have you got in?"

"Wow – you figured out that I am applying? Of course, you did. Yep, I also got a nomination from

Senator Javiss, along with a congressional nomination. I just finished the physical tests at Geiger Air Force Base. Everything is looking very positive, though I'm sure the blood tests aren't done yet."

"Don't worry," Ethan smiled. "Your skin is clearly not as pale as mine so no chance of my bad genes. But what about football? If you make it into West Point you will have to try out for the team as a walk-in. And I heard about the Seahawks."

Ben found himself again surprised at Ethan's perceptions. This man somehow was able to focus on the deep thoughts of his heart.

"Football," Ben sighed. "Yeah, this season is going super at WSU and I am only a sophomore. The interest from the Seahawks is heady, and very tempting. But it would be a bigger honor to play for West Point. Like you said though – my chances of playing quarterback for Army may be slim. The funny thing is that almost everyone thinks that my life revolves around that little pigskin."

Ben had a fleeting thought to change the conversation back to Katelyn but the whole conversation was freeing up some hidden passion. His excitement grew with each word.

"There are new skills I'm sure I can learn if I finish out college or head to the pros, but football no longer holds the same interest to me as it did several years ago," he continued. "This may sound corny, but I think you'll get it – you caught on to my love of strategy, didn't you? I want to learn strategies that save lives and protect my country. I think I have something to offer."

"So, the Seahawks and University of Washington are far second choices?" Ethan asked.

"You heard about U-dub?" Ben asked. "Oh yes – probably from Kat. And the Seahawks would be a fabulous opportunity, no doubt about it. It's a…plan." The silence stretched out as Ben pondered his future paths.

"There is always just enlisting," Ethan said. "With your smarts and energy, you could make it into one of the several high-tech military departments after basic training."

Ben turned to stare at Ethan in amazement. "How do you do that?" he asked. "How do you know the plans churning in my head?"

"We are kind of alike," Ethan said. "Except I played a real sport – soccer." Ben threw a handful of hay at him. "I don't have your peripheral vision but I bet I could take you in the 100-meter dash," Ethan challenged with a laugh.

"I seriously doubt it seeing I tied the WSU 100-meter record. If you could beat me, I'd know your secret."

"Yeah?" Ethan asked with a curious uplift of his dark, bushy eyebrows.

"Super pale skin, fast, dark wavy hair, and dark eyes – an Edward wanna-be if ever I saw one. Yeah, you would prove you're a vampire," said Ben.

"OK team Jacob, it's a little embarrassing that we both know the Twilight story characters," Ethan laughed. As they both settled backwards on the hay bales in the trailer, Ethan brought the conversation around to the issue they had been skirting all afternoon.

"What do we do about Katelyn?"

6. Evening Prayer

Ben's first thoughts were sobering. *How could Ethan talk about "we" and what was there to "do"?* As they faced each other across the trailer, Ben felt the initial gulf between them from the stables return with a vengeance.

Ethan settled backwards, leaning into a more casual pose, but he didn't release Ben's stare. After a moment Ethan reached and clasped both hands behind his head. Both men spoke volumes with their face and posture.

Ben finally asked, "You like her, don't you?"

"Yes," Ethan responded almost immediately. "You haven't told her about West Point yet, have you?"

"No. I'm sure it didn't take a chess grandmaster to figure that one out."

"Ben – months of planning and work, and probably years of thinking about the Academy and it never came up in conversation?" Ethan asked.

Ben sighed. "You have probably just started to get to know her, but she isn't an easy one to talk to. It got worse … several years ago." Ben halted. He suddenly felt vulnerable. Guilt seeped through his conscience for sharing about Katelyn.

What is it about this guy that draws out stuff that I haven't shared with anybody?

Ethan acted like he didn't catch the sudden stop in the conversation. Ben calmed a little at Ethan's silence but then his breath caught with Ethan's surprising next words.

"Really? A girlfriend of over five years and you can't help her enough through her own pain to give her the truth of who you are? The football quarterback and the hottest girl on campus. What is she to you? Another mountain to conquer and then move on from?"

Ben's eyes flared red, while the distance he had been trying to hold back settled between them again. "You have no right to talk to me like that!" he spit back at Ethan.

Ethan didn't reply. He just leaned over sideways to lay down across several bales while chewing on a straw. Ben stiffened as he watched Ethan's strange behavior. Finally, Ben unclenched his fists to Ethan's silent but unrelenting stare and put his unusual mind to work about the stark words that Ethan had spoken.

The truth clicked in his heart so loud that he imagined Ethan could hear it. Ben settled back onto the hay from his half-raised stance and relaxed his fists. This was not about challenging him for Katelyn. It was not even about his apparent fear of confronting Katelyn with new college plans. In just a short conversation, Ethan had somehow wormed his way into Ben's thinking and put his finger on the real priority Ben had been skirting for some time: Katelyn's feelings. Ben noticeably relaxed and thought through his reply.

"None of my friends would dare get in my face like this," Ben said. "Of course, they all know I would punch their lights out if they tried," he said through a wry smile.

Ethan let his humorous face surface again at Ben's words. Both men looked intently at each other.

Ben felt that Ethan's question required a response, and he surprised himself by opening up again. "I don't have a good answer to your question right now," Ben said. "I am more than ready to tell Katelyn, but now waiting for the right timing is the plan. Waiting actually feels harder."

Ethan nodded and said, "I know. Waiting is hard."

Ben just nodded to himself and looked down, missing the changing expressions that came over Ethan's face. Ethan glanced up into the sky briefly and his normally smiling face changed to thoughtful, then lit up with even more excitement, before returning to his unique grin.

After several moments of silence Ethan said, "Truly Benjamin, you are a man after God's own heart."

Wow – that seems a little strange, Ben thought, but from what I know of this guy already, typical. His words do strike my heart, though.

Ben replied, a little embarrassed, "Let's finish this job. I need to get back and check on my gang of painters."

Ben jumped down to the ground and clasped Ethan's hand firmly to help him down. They held their grip for a few seconds and then broke away. There were no more words to say right now – just a lot of thinking. Ben's emotions were flip-flopping between anger and empathy over Ethan's story and actions. And, Ben had no idea where to go with Ethan's words from the stable. One look from Ben was all it usually took for anybody thinking of wiling Katelyn away from him to turn and run. It had only happened a couple of times. Ethan – well he seemed another story.

Ben asked Ethan one more question, though he already knew the answer. "This is just between us for now?"

"Of course," Ethan answered.

Ethan put his ear buds back in and listened to his music as they continued to load the second trailer with the remaining hay bales. They finished and Ethan hooked up both trailers in a row as Ben operated the tractor. Ben looked down at Ethan from the tractor seat and nodded as he readied to leave. It was too noisy to say anything but their glances indicated the start of an unexpected friendship. Ben put the tractor in gear and drove to the pasture area while Ethan headed back to the main stables.

Josh, one of the younger stable hands, was back from the fields and already working in the stalls as Ethan walked into the barn.

"Hi, Ethan. Good to see you again."

"And you too, Josh."

"Janet sent me back to help you do a final clean-up since she will be tied up the rest of the afternoon with the girl who was helping you."

Ethan knew Josh from working together previously on some earlier private trips to the ranch.

They both were experts at taking a bad joke and keeping it going with additional puns, and immediately shared new gags. Within a short time, they finished with the special bedding in all the remaining stalls, and handled the horses returning with the other ranch hands, all to a continual banter of puns and wisecracks. The other workers left as soon as they could, not bearing to hear the awful non-stop jokes.

The sun had just set over the western hills when Ethan and Josh washed the tools and closed the stable. A few purplish-gray clouds that had settled over the far distant peaks began to turn multiple shades of red, orange, and pink as they walked back to clean up. They both had exhausted their repertoire of bad jokes and silently enjoyed the brilliant evening sky, which contrary to Janet's hints, promised to usher in a gorgeous day tomorrow.

"Good working with you, Ethan," Josh remarked as he parted company at the main lodge entrance, heading to the ranch-hand cabins. "You need to work on those puns, if you want to be more 'haylarious,'" he threw over his shoulder.

Ethan just smiled, letting Josh have the last joke. He bounded up the main lodge entry steps, through the empty common sitting area, and up the stairs surrounding the dining room hall. Dinner smells assaulted his nose and made his stomach gurgle as he entered his room on the second floor.

He showered in the guys' common bathroom, changed, and headed back down, charging directly to the counters where the food had already been laid out. He grabbed a tray, filled it overflowing with chicken, vegetables, and mashed potatoes and looked for a place to sit. He headed over to the only empty spaces at the cafeteria tables, which happened to be across from where Ben and Natalie were seated, already eating.

"May I join you?" Ethan asked. Ben hardly looked up from his food and gave Ethan a positive nod while continuing to eat. As Ethan sat down, Natalie began complaining to Ben.

"Slow down, Ben. If you spray me with gravy from that shovel, you call a fork, I'll baptize you with my ranch dressing," she quipped.

Ben looked up and gave her a silly look while he exaggerated chomping on his salad.

Natalie tried to look disgusted at Ben's loud chewing, but laughed instead. She looked over the table to Ethan and said, "Hi, you're Ethan – right?" There was no time for Ethan to chew his food and give an answer so he just gave a quick nod. "I'm Natalie, but most people call me Nat. So, where's Kat? Weren't you two working together in the stables?"

"Nat, will you let the poor guy eat?" Ben mumbled, helping himself to potatoes off Natalie's plate. Natalie tried to spear him with her fork but missed, getting it stuck in the lacquered wooden table.

"That could have hurt, Nat!" Ben exclaimed looking at the fork quivering in the table. Several of the other students at the table echoed Ben's surprise.

"You think?" Natalie replied. Ben watched Ethan's amusement at their joking and felt slightly embarrassed for Natalie. He knew there was no chance she could have actually stuck him, but her actions seemed unusual.

Natalie turned away from Ben as if the entire episode never happened and asked Ethan again, "So, where is Katelyn?"

Ethan had time to swallow his first couple of bites so he answered, "She spent most of the afternoon with Janet and the vet. She must not be back yet."

Natalie returned a slight smile at the word "vet." She just then noticed Katelyn entering the other side of the large dining hall from the side mud room.

Natalie stood and waved for her to join them but Katelyn shook her head, and began climbing the stairs, gesturing a need to change out of her dirty clothes.

Natalie sat down and noticed immediate tension at the table as Ethan and Ben had both stopped eating. Ethan had turned, and with a curious expression, watched Katelyn go up the stairs, meeting her glances back at the table several times. Ben peered at Ethan then Katelyn with a similar undecipherable gaze.

Natalie nudged Ben and arched her eyes in an unspoken question. Ben gave Natalie a side glance that said, "Don't ask."

The rest of the meal continued quietly with all three focused on their plates. Ethan finished first, stood, and said goodnight.

"Hope to see you at the service tonight," Natalie said to Ethan before he left the table. "It was nice meeting you."

"Thanks," replied Ethan. "I have one last chore to do but I'll try to make it."

He and Ben exchanged friendly nods. Ethan then walked over to the kitchen wash area and dropped off his tray. He steered his way around several tables towards the hallway heading to the main ranch entrance.

Natalie glanced at Ben, but before she spoke Ben said, "I said don't ask, Nat."

"Fine," she huffed. "But, for the record you didn't tell me the first time – you just gave me your quarterback glare. All right, here is a related question," she continued. "Why is Kat's father darting up from the table and making a bee-line intercept for our former dinner companion?"

Ben watched Gerald Braselli stand up from his table with the other adult youth group advisors and take long strides out of the dining room, intently focused upon the vanishing Ethan. He did not hurry, but Ben knew he moved with a determined purpose.

With a slightly sick look Ben turned to Natalie. "I'm not sure Nat, but you might want to pray."

Natalie's eyes squinted in concern. "Ben, what's going on?" she whispered to him.

"Even though Braz is on the youth board, this is the first ministry trip I have ever seen him come on, and he caught me by surprise with some questions about Ethan. They seemed innocent, but now that I think about them, they weren't so innocent after all. I forgot how good a lawyer he is and how he can weasel out the truth from hints and innuendos."

"So, what's the problem? Did you give him the impression that Ethan is an axe murderer? He sure seems a gentle soul to me."

"He is a good guy, but we are working out some private stuff right now."

Natalie's eyebrows raised. "About Kat, right?"

Ben turned and looked at her with haunted eyes. Instead of probing Ben further she said, "Then, let's pray right now."

Without waiting for an answer Natalie took his hand, leaned in, and prayed softly out loud. Ben's troubled heart settled, as Natalie, with no knowledge of Ethan and Ben's conversation, spoke a heartfelt request for comfort and insight around the very themes of their talk this afternoon.

"That was beautiful, Nat," Ben said when she finished.

Natalie leaned back, surprised, and asked, "Ben, what's happening to you? Requesting prayer for something other than football? Concern for somebody you barely know? And Ben, do you want to pray about something else?" she said, looking down at her hand still engulfed in Ben's.

A look of worry flashed across Ben's face, while Natalie's eyes widened in surprise.

"Hey you two, what's happening?" Katelyn asked, waltzing up to the table. They both quickly returned their hands to the table top. "Were you guys praying about something? Ben – you praying? I have got to hear this. I'll get my food and you guys can tell me all about it. I can't wait to share my day. I got to work with the veterinarian and it was great."

The unexpected exuberance of Katelyn's words did not erase the surprise on Natalie's face. As Katelyn practically danced over to the food line, Natalie glanced at Ben, who was also trying to calm his mixed feelings.

Natalie stood and said, "Ben, I just remembered I volunteered to help clean up. Tell Kat I'll catch her at the service."

Ben gave Natalie an annoyed look as she quickly retreated. "Hang in there, Ethan," he spoke to the silence, but his prayer was as much for himself as for his potential new friend...

7. Opportunities

Ethan was putting on his padded vest when Katelyn's father caught up to him.

"Excuse me. Ethan - wait," he said as Ethan turned around. "I am..."

"Mr. Braselli," Ethan interrupted, stretching out his hand. "It's a pleasure to meet you."

Gerald Braselli was accustomed to doing the interrupting, not being interrupted. His tall, athletic frame, perfectly coiffed silver-streaked hair, and sharp Italian features gave him a commanding presence, but beneath the polished exterior was a courtroom brawler. He left unprepared district attorneys and dishonest witnesses in tatters, relentless in his pursuit of the truth. His probing blue-green eyes, strikingly similar to Katelyn's, were always on the hunt for any weakness or deception.

"Please call me, 'Braz'," he said to Ethan as they exchanged a firm handshake. "Do you have some time to talk right now?" he asked, gesturing to the brightly lit foyer. The wide-open area was filled with western-style couches and over-stuffed chairs, dominated by a huge river-stone fireplace.

As people drifted in to sit by the fireplace and relax, Ethan replied, "Yes, but would you like to go somewhere a little more private? I was just walking up to the studio to check on something. We should be alone there."

"Sounds good," Braz said. "Lead the way." He grabbed a spare wool-lined overcoat from the front hall coat rack and followed Ethan out the massive main lodge doors.

Ethan pointed to a side path that led around the building. They followed the flagstone steps behind the dining hall until they turned into a wide bark-filled path heading up a hill, edged with large river rocks. Their frosty breaths hung in the moist resinous air. They both trudged silently over the bark and pine-needles, occasionally stepping over or kicking large pine cones. Tall cedar and ponderosa trees stood like gray sentinels along the path. Several widely-spaced, old-fashioned lamp posts lined the trail, providing small bubbles of yellow light to the dark walkway.

The path led up to a huge boulder and then split into two wide opposite trails, both continuing up the hill. Ethan, a few steps ahead of Braz, headed up the left fork without slowing. Braz looked up the path Ethan chose and could see a small porchlight in the distance.

Several minutes later they arrived at a plateau on the hillside, cleared of fir trees, and housing an angular-sided, tall one-story building with a single light over the porch entrance. Braz could not judge the size of the building from the angles and darkness. Ethan unlocked the door and flipped on the lights. They walked into a good-sized entryway, lit by wall lamps and decorated with a feminine flair: on either side were padded benches with flowered pillows, while interspersed on the warm-colored walls were many black and white photos of dancers on a stage. Opposite the entry door and its side windows were a pair of frosted glass French Doors with lace shears.

"We need to wear either slippers or socks inside," Ethan said, motioning to multiple pairs of moccasins and slippers under the benches. After changing footwear, Braz followed Ethan through the French Doors. Braz looked around in amazement as Ethan turned on the wall lamps.

Sixteen-foot-high cream-colored walls enclosed a large octagon-shaped room. Narrow floor-to-ceiling windows lined several of the walls, while one wall had a huge flat-screen television, and another had a huge framed mirror with a ballet barre mounted in front. Padded benches were scattered under most of the windows. The wall lamps reflected soft golden hues off the immaculately polished wooden floor. A huge chandelier hung from the center of the domed ceiling. As Ethan turned on the chandelier and adjusted it to a low level, the light exposed a hand-troweled plaster ceiling, tinted pale blue, and domed in the middle to over twenty feet.

"I did not imagine this when you said studio," Braz said as he walked his eyes around the perimeter. "Besides the beautiful craftsmanship, this is something I would expect in a Seattle loft apartment, not at a Montana horse ranch. Is someone a dancer?" Braz asked, focusing on the ballet barre.

"Janet's mother, Teresa," Ethan answered. "She was in a ballet troupe and taught for many years. Teresa's husband built this for her. It's a unique room, isn't it? I love coming up here in the evening when the setting sun breaks through the trees and lights up the room. And," Ethan smiled, "the acoustics in this room are awesome. I've cranked up the volume till the chandelier shakes."

"I'm not interrupting your plans, am I?" Braz asked.

"No, not at all. I just need to check the sound system. Janet said it has been crackling lately."

"Can I help?"

"Actually, you can." Ethan walked over to one of the side walls near the main double doors and pushed on a normal looking decorative panel. The entire panel opened revealing multiple electronic components on racks and oiled oak shelving. Various red and green lights blinked from a modem and some of the other audio mixers.

Ethan slowly pulled out one large amplifier from off its shelf and asked Braz to hold it while he checked the rear connections. He located a loose ground wire, the only cable not using an adaptor plug, and tightened it down. Ethan turned on the main power and adjusted the volume knob several times.

"Yep, no crackling," Ethan remarked. "I thought that might be the problem. I'll double-check it tomorrow."

Ethan took the amplifier from Braz and gently slid it back into position. Closing the panel, Ethan led Braz over to one of the corners, where several worn leather chairs sat over a thick Persian rug, framing a modern propane wall fireplace. Ethan switched on the fire, which cast a warm glow into the room.

Ethan and Braz settled back in the soft chairs as the firelight danced in the many reflections off the darkened windows on either side of the fireplace.

"So, Ethan," Braz started. "What are your intentions with my daughter, Katelyn?"

Ethan looked at Braz with some surprise. Inwardly, Braz smiled. Clearly, he caught Ethan unprepared with his direct approach.

"You are considering evading my question," Braz stated, watching Ethan pause.

"No," Ethan simply said.

As Braz stared intently at Ethan, he considered that he may have misread the young man. His simple reply echoed truth. Ethan did not move his hands from his lap, furtively look around the room, or perform any of the myriad tell-tale signs of someone preparing to lie that Braz had come to expect from many years of interrogating witnesses in the courtroom.

"Katelyn is very precious to me," Ethan answered quietly. "I would never do anything to hurt her," he replied with greater boldness.

Braz remained still, recognizing the sincerity in the reply, and that Ethan was working hard to find the right words. The word "precious," however, was daunting.

"Today was a great day, sir," Ethan continued, breaking into a grin. "I began to really know Katelyn as we worked together in the stables. She has a beautiful spirit and some special dreams."

"And some definite plans," Braz offered, now with more curiosity than challenge.

Ethan gave a reply that drove to the heart of the issue Braz seemingly raised.

"I also got to know Benjamin for the first time today. I believe we started a good friendship. I wouldn't do anything that jeopardized his and Katelyn's relationship."

"Huh," Braz said, not really convinced. "And her college plans?"

Ethan raised his eyebrows in response. His look revealed to Braz that the importance of Katelyn's law school plans wasn't something Ethan had weighed as serious. Braz watched Ethan trying to arrange his thoughts. Ethan looked like his mind was somewhere else.

After a minute Ethan replied, "Well, certainly, that too."

Braz read the truth in Ethan's response but caught the hint of something deeper, unsaid. There was something unique about this curious young man. Abandoning his plan to be the father-lawyer, Braz relaxed, and decided upon a different approach.

"I tend to overprotect Katelyn, raising her as a single parent," Braz said. "I've noticed you off and on at church over the years, where you have never been involved with the activities of your age group, let alone connect with my daughter. Since you joined us here on the retreat you seem to be very focused on her. Anything you'd like to share?"

Again, Ethan reacted differently than Braz envisioned. Instead of asking how Braz was aware of Ethan and Katelyn's day, he stood up, walked to the nearest floor-to-ceiling window, and peered into the darkness. His facial expressions changed several times, and Braz thought he saw Ethan's lips moving in his reflection on the glass.

"I don't have any sisters," he finally spoke into the window. "And, I was raised by an aunt, so I have never seen how a man watches over his daughter. I can imagine the difficulty, especially without a wife, but I only understand a little where you're coming from." Ethan turned back and faced Braz. "All I have to offer you is the truth of my experiences and hope it answers your questions."

"Alright," Braz answered. "Please continue."

Ethan headed over and sit again in the leather chair. Braz recognized that Ethan had come to some decision; he had the same look when witnesses in the courtroom let go of their evasions to reveal the truth. He began speaking, alternating his glances between Braz and the fireplace.

"When I first met Katelyn, a little over four years ago in high school, I was overwhelmed by her beauty." Ethan smiled at the memory.

"Our socializing was minimal, her being a sophomore, clearly involved with a football player, and my being a new student ready to graduate. But, in the little things I observed, and our casual interactions, I saw that her intelligence, determination, and gentle heart were just as beautiful."

"You were smitten," Braz interrupted.

Ethan confirmed Braz's perception with a broader smile. "College was going to take me away from Spokane when I graduated, probably for good, and Katelyn's and Ben's relationship was evident and special."

Again, Ethan slightly paused.

He certainly is a man who thinks out his words, Braz thought.

"I set aside my feelings."

Braz saw that there was some pain behind that last simple statement but didn't press him to explain more. Braz was growing more surprised that Ethan was revealing a depth to his heart to a practical stranger. A part of Braz wondered if this was some ploy.

"After my plans changed and I stayed in Washington, it still didn't seem right to approach her," Ethan continued. "I didn't have the wisdom, and I still don't, on how to orchestrate a connection with her that does not hurt her relationship with Ben. So, I waited."

Braz was slightly stunned. He clearly heard the truth behind Ethan's words, and was amazed that Ethan appeared to be more concerned about Katelyn than himself, especially with hints of the depth of his own feelings.

Again, as Braz watched Ethan stare into the fire, Ethan seemed to be holding a conversation with someone else. Ethan's hidden musing irritated Braz. Though Ethan's revelations were more than he had ever expected to hear from this conversation, Braz's aggravation got the better of him. The lawyer-father returned and blurted out a challenge.

"But now you are making your move."

"Some things are not what they appear," Ethan said.

"Your interactions with her this weekend are an accident, then?" Braz continued with raised eyebrows. The lawyer was now fully back.

Braz watched Ethan's entire posture relax. Ethan turned his head towards Braz and showed his quirky grin. Braz tried to control his widening eyes as Ethan began talking about someone else, with even greater delight. Ethan's words cut through Braz's cynicism like a knife.

"I am simply telling you that I feel a freedom to connect with her, but not from a calculated plan," Ethan said. "I trust that the circumstances that are presenting themselves are opportunities from someone with much more wisdom than I."

"Really?" Braz did not look convinced, but for one of the few times in his life he had run out of words. Ethan appeared to want to say more but did not offer any more explanations.

After several minutes of silence Ethan stood and said, "I hope you don't mind stopping here, but I would like to drop by and talk to Janet before it's too late."

"Very well," Braz said. "I'll turn off the fireplace and you hit the lights."

Heading back out into the evening air, they both tightened up their collars – the night colder than when they had arrived. Braz took the lead this time trudging down the hillside. Ethan interrupted their trek when they reached the large boulder, and reached his hand out to Braz.

"Janet's place is up the other trail here," Ethan said. "Thanks. It has been a pleasure. Katelyn is indeed a most beautiful woman," he softly spoke. "I have thanked the Lord for the chance just to get to know her this weekend."

Braz gave a parting shot as he released Ethan's strong handshake: part apology, part serious father.

"Get to know her better, Ethan. But, if you hurt her, I'll have no mercy for you."

Ethan returned his standard smile. "Patience is my middle name Mr. Braselli. But, just to let *you* know – if the opportunity arises to show her my real affection, I'll do just that!"

Ethan then immediately turned before Braz could reply and headed up the other trail, his lengthy strides moving him towards a large modern cedar log cabin, lit up and peeking through the trees.

Braz watched him go for a moment and then turned and resumed his hike back down to the main lodge. He pursed his lips with a worried frown. As he pondered Ethan's openness and audacity he spoke into the night.

"An honest man who thinks he hears from God. Heaven help us from what he will stir up!"

8. A Crack in the Door

Katelyn shuffled into the barely-lit cafeteria kitchen and was greeted by a voice from the darkened corner.

"Good morning, Katelyn. You are up early." Ethan's words and broad smile greeted Katelyn as she reached for the simmering coffee pot. "Are you on breakfast detail?" he continued, as he moved over to join her under the single-lit fluorescent light. "By the way, you look lovely in the morning."

Katelyn peeked through half-lidded eyes at Ethan as he walked over. She frowned at his remark, thinking he was just being sarcastic, and said, "Will you stop that?"

As she glanced at her old, oversized sweatshirt trailing over her flannel pajama bottoms, she continued, "I look a mess. And, no – I am not cooking breakfast." She narrowed her eyes further trying to minimize the harsh light in her face, and get out from it revealing her tousled hair and face without makeup. "Are you one of those perky morning people? If so, tell me in an hour."

Ethan laughed and followed her to a table in the dark and empty dining hall, lit only by the overflow light from the kitchen. Ethan watched quietly as she sipped her coffee.

"Umm. This is good," she said.

"Thanks. My special brew," Ethan said, and then shifted and stared off towards one of the dark windows. "Would you rather be alone?"

"S-fine," Katelyn mumbled as she peeked at Ethan over her cup.

"OK, but it's a little cold in here. How about moving to the foyer? The couches are a lot more comfortable than these chairs. I do have to leave in about 30 minutes to help round up some wayward stallions but I could restart the fire."

"That sounds nice."

Katelyn got up and followed Ethan into the foyer area lit only by a small night-light. Cold blackness poured through the windows as daybreak was still about an hour away. Ethan turned on a table lamp while Katelyn settled into the end of a large overstuffed leather couch near the fireplace. She covered her legs with one of the soft comforters folded in a nearby basket.

Ethan stirred up the banked embers and added some paper and kindling to get the fire burning in the large open pit area. After the kindling burned brightly, he added several pieces of chopped pine logs, replaced the standing screen, and sat down in the middle of the long couch. The larger logs started crackling and spitting as flames brightened up the dim room.

Remembering their conversation yesterday Katelyn asked, "I thought you didn't like to ride. How are you going help round up some of the herd?"

Ethan's face lit up. "Four-wheel ATV's. They're the modern pack horse and much more fun!"

Katelyn smiled slightly and returned to watch the fireplace while Ethan silently sipped his coffee.

Who is this quiet man? Katelyn asked herself. Should I bring up the question of his "opportunity" statement yesterday?

Instead, Katelyn just quietly sighed, and then broke the silence with a several wide yawns. Ethan turned to her with just a little concern on his face.

"I didn't sleep well last night," she answered to Ethan's silent stare. He responded only with a caring lift of his head.

"As a matter of fact, I don't think I slept at all," she continued more softly.

"You Ok? Want to talk about it?"

"No, I don't want to talk about it," she replied rather harshly. This conversation was going in the opposite direction of where she intended. She did not want to relive the painful discussion she had with Ben last night. Ethan just slightly nodded.

"Who taught you how to listen so well?" Katelyn rubbed her eyes to make sure they didn't tear up.

"Comes from being raised by a very intelligent and outgoing aunt, with nobody else in the household — she has lots of words."

After a pause, Katelyn asked, "No parents?"

"They both passed away when I was in middle school. Aunt Desirée is my mom's sister, and works as a nurse at Sacred Heart Hospital. She was awesome at filling the gap, though. She is more than just my aunt now — she is my best friend."

Katelyn, nearly choking, looked at Ethan with sadness. "I'm sorry that you lost both your parents, Ethan. I don't know if I could have ever recovered from that, even with an aunt as special as yours."

She turned back to look at the brightly burning fireplace and tightened her grip on the comforter.

"My dad has done a good job, too, after we lost my mom."

Ethan inched over next to her, put his arm around her shoulders, and spoke softly, "Sometimes though - you need your mother."

Katelyn did not resist as Ethan pulled her gently close, and the tears she had successfully held off began raining from both eyes. After several minutes, Ethan pulled back and reached into his pocket and handed Katelyn a handkerchief. Katelyn, looked through clouded eyes with a questioning look.

"Unused – promise," he said.

As she cleaned herself up, Ethan returned to the center of the couch. His shifting away was appreciated by Katelyn, now slightly embarrassed, but something inside her slightly recoiled as feelings of loss painfully echoed in her heart.

Both continued to sit quietly and watch the igniting logs and growing flames paint wavering shadows around the room. The silence became deafening to Katelyn, but she did not want to give this man anything more; her tears were a weakness she had not planned on sharing. Yet, his brief hug was not condescending. He appeared to be clearly settled in his skin, and whether she cried or remained silent, he gave off a feeling of all is well.

But Ben – ugh! And now Ethan pulled away before I made him scoot over, she fumed. The only response to her seething was the gently crackling fireplace, and shifting of the logs, as Ethan apparently ignored her mounting frustration.

Whether it was anger or just a black need to challenge the man who clearly projected a listening ear and trustworthy heart, she finally broke the stillness with her words.

"Ben and I talked last night," she started.

Katelyn began to clench and unclench the comforter, while her breathing got faster. With eyes glued to the fireplace she took a long breath and hurled out her pain, ignoring a whining voice within her to not risk her heart on a man she barely knew.

"It was about what he mentioned yesterday when he saw us in the stables. He hopes to transfer to West Point next year, but I guess you know that already since he said that you two discussed that yesterday, before he ever shared with me. It makes a lot of sense and he is very happy about the possibility, which makes me happy too, but I don't know why he never shared that with me before, and why he let us make lots of plans for going to WSU, and now the possible move to Seattle, and all of a sudden I feel stupid because it's like I never knew him, and it wasn't like this in the beginning with all those years growing closer, and yet I never saw him changing, and I get the feeling that he is not telling me everything, and yes I'm mad, really mad, but it's mostly angry at myself for not seeing, and maybe I did this to him, and is there more he is not sharing, and I don't know if I want to hear it since it looks like another typical ruin in my life…"

"Katelyn," Ethan gently interrupted. "Breathe."

She stopped, sniffed several times, and used the handkerchief clutched in her other hand. "You wanted to go to West Point, too?" she asked after a couple of long breaths. "I remember you mentioning that to Ben in the stable yesterday."

"It was a life-long dream, but after it didn't happen, I realized something very important. It was more my father's dream than mine."

Ethan stopped. Katelyn glanced at him feeling like he wanted to say more, but could see that his focus was interrupted by something else.

She felt Ethan relax and turn to look at her. Again, ignoring the voice inside, now screaming for her to stop, she deliberately returned her stare to the flickering fire, and curiously asked, "And...?"

Ethan immediately responded, "A more precious dream has started to come true."

Without turning to watch him, Katelyn could sense that Ethan's face was alight with joy.

"I'm not ready for this talk, Ethan," she spoke into the fireplace, afraid to turn and see his face.

"Maybe not, and then maybe it's the perfect time."

Before she could object, Ethan softly said, "Katelyn, you have captivated my heart from the day I first saw you."

He stopped, his silence after that declaration drawing her own frustration to the surface.

She twisted to challenge his focus on her, alight with joy, and with more than just the flames of the fireplace reflected in her eyes, she erupted, "You know - I wonder why you look at me with those crazy grins, and how the personal things you say don't creep me out. It must be that Mr. Spock smile that is always on your face. There," she pointed. "Your right eyebrow does this weird thing and one part of your lip is crooked."

Ethan's eyes went wide.

"You have been noticing my rugged and handsome face. And you know about Star Trek! I knew you were special, and now I'm convinced!"

Despite the feelings swirling around her heart, Katelyn tried not to smile at the absurdity of Ethan's reaction. She just shook her head back and forth, as Ethan continued to smile his quirky grin.

The voice that had been screaming in her heart took over her mind again, releasing an oily satisfaction at Katelyn's lashing out. But, as Ethan's smile softened, Katelyn slowly ebbed into a familiar dullness. The slight smile that had begun with Ethan's ridiculous reply washed away to a grey weariness. The exclamation of Ethan's heart was all but forgotten.

Ethan watched the panoply of emotions across Katelyn's face and smoothed his own smile. He stood up as Katelyn reflexively wiped her dry eyes. He put his vest on over his heavy flannel shirt and said, "I have to go. You alright?"

Surprised at Ethan's abrupt departure, all she could manage through tight lips was a faint, "Better."

"Well, I know something that will make you feel more than better. If you finish in time with helping the vet today, come visit the studio around three this afternoon. Something special is going to take place there. It's just up the hill behind the main lodge. Stay left on the trail and you can't miss it."

"Alright," she answered, wiping her nose one last time. "I'll see."

"Great. Have fun today. I'll catch you later. Oh — and keep the handkerchief."

As Ethan walked out the door Katelyn wondered out loud. "How did you know I was helping the veterinarian today?" Ethan's unlooked-for revelation surfaced in her mind. And captivated! Who talks like that? And why did you just leave without explaining what you really mean?

She loosened the comforter, drawing it back to her lap, and tried to focus on Ethan's words but revelations from Ben last night kept intruding. Just as she was about to relive the entire painful conversation with Ben, Natalie entered the room in her old high school track sweat suit, large purple and pink fluff robe, and worn bunny-face slippers. She was carrying a cup of hot chocolate and yawning. Her short, auburn hair was sticking out at various angles. Katelyn couldn't help but smile at her bohemian friend.

"Yo Kat – 'mornin," Natalie said. "At least I think it is morning. You look like I feel," she blurted out and then plopped on the couch. "Thanks for keeping me up all night with your tossing and turning."

"Sorry," Katelyn replied and stopped without further comment.

Natalie continued as if not hearing the pain in Katelyn's voice. "Great. We get one of the few rooms with a bed that the Hulk slept in. That mattress has a crevice in the middle that would get a bowling ball rolling. Every time you moved, I felt like I was falling downhill."

"Were you cold last night, Nat?" Katelyn responded with obvious fake concern and a glimmer of a smile, arousing to the joy that followed Natalie around like a second skin. "I noticed you were wearing your wool socks. Every time you rolled in the middle, they touched my bare feet and started me itching."

"Oh – so now it's my fault? Tonight, I'm adding two extra comforters. I'll pile one in the middle so you can stay on your side."

They ribbed each other back and forth as the fire crackled, settling into the sharing that marked their deep friendship. It was a salve to Katelyn's feelings.

Natalie finally asked the question that Katelyn had expected.

"So, did you and Ben have a tough conversation last night after the service? What did he share that ruined your sleep – and mine?" she anxiously asked.

Katelyn responded, a lot calmer now from Ethan's caring concern and Nat's friendly banter. She first determined to get an answer for herself before satisfying Natalie's curiosity.

"When I sat down at the dinner table yesterday, Ben only gave me the barest facts about what you guys were praying about, and then gave me some silly excuse to beg out before we could talk further. I noticed my best friend had escaped, too."

Natalie took a sip of her hot chocolate. "Wow – Miss Lawyer Braselli. You just expertly evaded my question."

"Like you at dinner," Katelyn bounced back. "Alright, Ben and I did have a long conversation about college plans after the service. It was finally good to hear his heart, after so long at keeping it a secret, but…" Katelyn just sighed and stopped, dragging the silence out until only the crackling fire was the only sound in the room.

"Sure, go ahead and clam up," Natalie said. I'll show you who the better lawyer is. I'm sticking with you all day, girl. I'll drag it out of you."

Katelyn glanced over to Natalie and thanked her with amused eyes.

"Well don't think it's just about you," Natalie grimaced. "I need to get away from a certain college freshman here at the retreat. Nick."

"That skinny guy with glasses and a funny cowlick in his hair?" Katelyn asked. "He attends Whitman College, doesn't he? Now that I think about it, I have seen him try to sit near you at church the whole summer."

"Yeah. He found out we share a love of chemistry and somehow got on the same work detail yesterday. He wouldn't shut up about the periodic table, and how amazing that we share the same interests. I finally gave him some of my latest shampoo concoction and told him I wouldn't talk to him anymore unless he could identify the main ingredients."

"Frankincense and myrrh?" Katelyn asked with a chuckle.

"Shhh!" Natalie whispered, glancing around the empty room. "I hope it keeps him busy enough till we head back home. But it may backfire," she said forlornly. "He looked really excited about the challenge, and he might be smarter than I think."

"Come on," she said standing up and pulling the comforter away from Katelyn. "Let's get ready for breakfast before he comes down. And besides, you look terrible and will need a lot of work."

"Treat me nice, Nat, or I might slip Nick the answer," Katelyn warned, to which Natalie responded with an attempt to mess up her hair. Katelyn ran up the three flights of stairs to their room holding Natalie's hand, the pain barred and locked away once more.

9. *Dancing*

"Did Ethan say to go right or left?" Natalie asked as they trudged up the trail behind the main lodge.

"I'm sure he said left, but I might not be remembering his directions," Katelyn replied, peering around a giant boulder at two paths heading off almost opposite each other. Neither girl was breathing hard, being in great shape, but they were both tired from non-stop activity helping the vet check out multiple horses, in addition to not having slept much the night before. The crisp mountain air in late afternoon was filled with the scents of cedar, moss, and pine bark, but still failed to revive the tired girls.

"You sure you don't want to head down and relax in the lodge?" Natalie continued. "You still haven't given me the whole scoop of your talk with Ben - wait. Listen," she said, cocking an ear towards the left trail. "I hear faint music."

"I don't hear a thing," Katelyn said.

"Go left, O deaf one," Natalie pushed at Katelyn. "Now I'm curious. That sounds like one of the Hillsong-Live worship songs."

Both girls continued their climb up the trail. It ended at short wooden stairs leading up to a wide covered porch. The last remnants of fall flowers filled several large pots sitting next to two white-painted wooden rocking chairs on the veranda. The walls of the building angled back from the porch and they could see a couple of windows cracked open on one side.

Violins, flutes, and piano tones floated from the open windows, accompanied by a woman's voice. The music continued uninterrupted as Katelyn knocked on the door. When nobody answered, Natalie tried the door handle, peered into the entryway, and beckoned Katelyn to follow her. They entered a vestibule, brightly lit from the windows framing the entry door and an overhead skylight. A couple of coats were hung on pegs and they could see several stained boots tucked under the padded benches lining the wall. The music was clearly coming from the room beyond. Katelyn and Natalie could see some blurred forms moving around through the curtained windows on a pair of French Doors, opposite the entry door.

Before Natalie tried the French Doors, Katelyn tapped her on the shoulder and pointed to a rustic sign asking visitors to remove their shoes. Both girls hung up their coats, then sat down on the thickly cushioned side benches and removed their shoes.

Katelyn put on a pair of leather slippers while Natalie just padded over to the door in her thick wool socks.

They were just about to crack open the interior doors when they heard a sound like a herd of horses behind them. As they turned, they were surprised to see Ben and his two constant football companions, Chet and Brian, crash through the outside door.

"Beat you again, losers," Ben jeered, out of breath.

"We only let you win, so the quarterback doesn't lose his confidence," Brian gasped between breaths.

"Shh!" both girls whispered. "And take off your shoes if you are going to follow us in!"

"Ok," the boys said quietly and began removing their hiking boots.

"Why are we whispering?" Ben asked. "We won't disturb anyone with the music that loud."

Katelyn and Natalie ignored them as they opened the interior door and inched into the room. Ben and his friends followed. They all stopped immediately at the entrance. A figure in dark body tights, a short skirt, and flowing long blond hair was dancing in the middle of the large room to a music video displayed on the large display screen. The television was showing a

Hillsong worship leader singing "What a Beautiful Name," while the music blared from multiple hidden speakers.

As the dancer twirled, Katelyn was surprised to see that it was Janet. She was spinning in the middle of the polished wooden floor with a grace that left them all amazed. It was clear that she was focused on something beyond the music by the look on her face. As they watched Janet perform complicated bends, twists, and arm and leg rotations, they realized, with awe, that Janet was dancing with an unseen presence.

Katelyn saw a movement from the corner of her eye and turned to see Ethan standing in a corner. He was oblivious to their presence like Janet, as his head was raised with closed eyes. His body was slightly swaying while his hands moved in what looked like exaggerated sign language. He then began dancing, but it appeared more like slow motion martial arts. As he slowly turned, he opened his eyes and spied Katelyn and her friends at the entrance. He smiled and beckoned them in but didn't stop.

It was Ben, who surprising Katelyn, succumbed first to the invitation floating in the very air. As the music reached one of its first crescendos he started his own slow twirl, adding extreme stretching moves that only his powerful body could perform. His dancing slowly resulted in him joining Ethan till the two looked like they were locked in a slow-motion battle with hidden swords.

Katelyn glanced back and forth between Janet, Ethan, and Ben, and watched in awe as they all moved with a beautiful grace, entranced with the lovely music and powerful words.

Katelyn and Natalie gave each other a glance. This kind of devotion was something they had never done before, but Janet's dancing, and now the two men enraptured with quiet expressions, beckoned them to join. They both shyly moved forward and then twirled into the room near Janet with raised hands. Somehow, the atmosphere in the room affected Ben's two friends also, and they enthusiastically joined the other men, adding their own unique arm and hand moves to the dance. It felt to Katelyn that her feet were no longer on the floor, and her eyes closed from a peace that reverberated off the walls with every note.

The video ended and they all slowed, but then the video playlist moved on to another powerful worship song. All again took up their dance steps, first more gently, and then with increased vigor. Chet stopped and moved over to the window, pulled out his cell phone and tapped a couple of texts, and then rejoined the others.

As the song ended, Janet glided over to Katelyn and Natalie, and without stopping, took their hands, finishing out the song as a circling trio. The next song then started and Janet kept them flowing, the three of them moving like a dance team: switching hands, pirouetting, and bowing.

The horns and synthesizer started increasing in volume with another song as the French Doors opened. Several heads from the college youth group peeked in. When they saw the others dancing, they shrugged off any inhibition and entered the room with smiles and vigor. Some joined the dancing in the center of the floor while others moved to the edges and started worshipping just with lifted hands.

Several songs later the music ended with the group on the video clapping in praise. As the room grew quiet, everyone looked around. Katelyn was surprised that over an hour had passed since they had arrived, and that practically the entire group of young adults were there.

Katelyn looked at Janet next to her and said with flushed cheeks, "We have never worshipped like this before. It was beautiful. You were beautiful."

Janet replied looking around her, trying to catch the eye of everyone. "And so were all of you!" she said.

As most of the young people rested to catch their breath, Janet continued with an impromptu sharing. "Long ago, a king was caught up in a similar expression like what you have done today. His heart was so full of love and joy that he lost all propriety of being king to dance in the presence of his Lord, without his formal robes and crown."

"I know that story," Katelyn interrupted. "It was King David, wasn't it? He was bringing the Ark of the Covenant to its resting place in Jerusalem."

"Yes," Janet smiled back to Katelyn. "But we have something now that King David could only dream about. He danced alone, but we have each other." Janet spun with arms extended, as if trying to embrace the whole crowd.

"And we are not just a people carrying the presence of God over a box," she continued. "No, not just a Lord with us…," she paused.

A light flickered in Katelyn's eyes, and a thought bubbled up from somewhere to finish Janet's thought.

But before she could express it one of the other students blurted out, "Is there some more? We just got here."

"Of course," Janet beamed. She glanced over to Ethan to give him a look, but he was already moving over to the electronics cabinet.

Katelyn held her breath as the thought of completing Janet's statement drifted out of her mind. The words were so right and amazing. She tried to say them aloud but it was like trying to grasp a wisp of smoke. All that was left was a sense of wonder. Sadness threatened to overwhelm her as she felt a loss of an unknown treasure.

As Ethan turned on a video of worship at a church, in Redding, California, Katelyn entered back into the joyous exuberance of the group, but could not get her mind off the forgotten answer. I need to talk with Janet alone, she thought.

Katelyn's mood brightened and the feeling of a great loss receded as the music began to swell. Each one in the studio began to move to their own individual vision, and then the entire group began to move in a unity that caught everyone in a grip of love. This feeling continued through the worship set and spontaneous worship. As the music faded most looked around with faces full of smiles.

Ethan, still next to the electronics cabinet, turned off the display with the ending of the worship video and started a music mix from his phone. This time the feeling in the entire room switched to uncontained joy as praise songs, filled with bass and drums, bounced off the ceiling. The smiles broadened around the room as the group naturally all moved together into the center of the room, with Ethan and Ben coming up next to Katelyn. They all laughed at each other as their heads bobbed to the beat, and voices echoed the words blaring from the speakers.

First voices, then hands, and then heads were raised in joyous song. It only took a few minutes before Katelyn took off her slippers and threw them over the heads of the group towards the wall. She then started leaping straight into the air. It then became a joyous romp as socks and footwear began flying across the room while everyone began jumping. Katelyn and Ethan quickly got separated in the energetic crowd. People moved off to the side benches to rest as the songs continued but couldn't help themselves and joined back in with the group after a few moments.

Suddenly the lights flickered off and on and the music abruptly stopped. Everyone looked around in surprise, trying to catch their breaths. Katelyn looked around back to the electronic console but instead of

Ethan saw Josiah, the college youth pastor, and several of the adult youth advisors. Josiah had a scowl on his face while most of the other adults looked angry. Katelyn saw that fortunately her father was not with the advisor group. Josiah's scowl deepened when he recognized Kara, the daughter of the church head pastor, and his fiancé, in the middle of the floor, bent over catching her breath.

"This is really disappointing," Josiah spoke loudly. "I thought we had some discussions about this kind of behavior." Josiah looked around at the red-faced and sweaty group, some still bent over, breathing heavy, and looked disapprovingly at the piles of socks, sweaters, and shirts strewn about the walls. His eyes searched for Katelyn, specifically, and finding her, tightened his lips in quiet condemnation.

"And what would our host think?" one of the adults asked, disgustedly. "You all need to leave immediately and get cleaned up for dinner."

As the embarrassed group silently picked up their clothes and moved to the doors, Janet walked up to one of the side hooks, grabbed a towel, and slowly followed the chagrined students. She tried to smile at Katelyn and Natalie, but neither woman could lift their eyes from the floor.

Katelyn finally stood up on her toes trying to catch a glimpse of Ethan. She couldn't see him in the press of everyone funneling out. Janet meanwhile had stopped in front of the advisors, whom, along with Josiah, tried to cover their surprise. Katelyn, right behind Janet, almost ran into her as Janet paused.

"The host does know, and only has the deepest respect for young people who can abandon themselves to praise and worship like this," Janet said.

"You encouraged this, Janet?" Josiah asked, gently grabbing the arm of Kara as she tried to slip by.

The other advisors quickly recovered and put on stern faces as Janet said, "I usually practice around this time if I can get away. It is a wonderful time of worship. I welcome any who want to join."

"Well, it didn't look like worship to me," one man growled. "It looked more like a rock concert."

Katelyn edged her way closer to Janet's side for support. Janet pulled the towel over her shoulders and both silently exchanged the same thought, imagining the stern gentleman at a rock concert, crowd surfing in the mosh pit. Katelyn successfully kept her lips pressed together but Janet could not hold back her smile.

"This is not funny, young lady," the advisor said. I had reservations about our group travelling this far but didn't expect to find us having to guard our students from such...influences. Looks like Katelyn's idea of coming here was a bad choice. Worse, I now seem to remember a similar incident many years ago."

He turned to Josiah and continued, "We need to reconsider our contract and discuss leaving tomorrow instead of Sunday," he said with a determined scowl. He gathered the other church advisors with a head nod and walked out the door. "Coming Josiah?" he asked, looking back.

"Yes. I'll meet with you before dinner." Josiah walked with his fiancé in tow over to one of the side benches and quietly started berating her.

Natalie had already left, so Katelyn slunk through the door after the advisors, shoulders bowed, alone, but stopped with Janet in the vestibule, as a ranch worker entered with a worried frown.

Roberto, the head hand at the ranch, wormed his way towards Janet, not too gently through the fleeing advisors, hearing the end of their rebuke. As he came up to Janet, his frown had turned to scowling.

Janet laid a gentle touch on his arm and quietly said, "It's Ok, Roberto. These judgements do not bother me."

"Well, they bother me, miss. But regardless, they are going nowhere. You were right; the storm has shifted and is moving faster than forecasted. Lookout Pass is closed. The highway is almost impassable at Missoula and there are several inches of snow already on the ground at Butte. The weather service is saying it will start snowing here in a couple of hours, with possibly three to four feet. They warned of major drifts with the winds."

Janet's eyebrows raised in alarm.

"Before you start worrying," he continued, "I have already begun moving the two main herds into the lower pastures."

"You will need some help to get as many of the younger horses we can to shelter," Janet quickly replied moving towards the door, with Roberto hurrying to keep up. "We also need to check the propane generators in case we lose power." Their voices continued as they left the building, discussing plans to protect the guests and animals. They were so engrossed in their planning neither saw Katelyn, remaining behind.

Katelyn eased up behind the open French Doors and peered through the crack seeing only Kara and Josiah left in the room. She watched as Kara stood up, sobbing, and ran out of the room, and then ran outside too quickly for Katelyn to grab her and give her some comfort. Katelyn pierced her lips together and her eyes squinted. Her cheeks flushed even redder from the initial embarrassment as anger began pulsing faster through her whole body.

Ben, advisors, and now Josiah! God, how could you allow another ruin? she screamed to herself.

She steeled herself to barge in and confront the latest disappointment in her life and at least get some satisfaction for Kara. Just as she grabbed the door handle, she glimpsed another figure in the room. It was Ethan! Katelyn froze and moved back to get a clearer view. Ethan walked up to the electronics closet and retrieved his phone and then wandered over and stood beside Josiah.

"Josiah, do you have a minute for me to show you something that will really bless you?" Ethan asked.

Katelyn took a breath. Why would Ethan want to bless Josiah? I would like to throttle him. Who is this man?

10. New Vistas

Josiah answered with a disgusted face locked on the floor. "First the chaperones, then the whole youth group, and now the girl of my dreams - who it looks like I'm farther away from marrying, especially when her father finds out the mess I let happen."

Katelyn silently smiled but immediately felt guilty.

Ethan watched Josiah for a couple of seconds, then walked over to the panel controls. He activated the huge video screen and connected a streaming link from his phone. Soft music began playing as the screen displayed a ballet dancer moving around a stage in slow twirls. Though the quality of the video was grainy, the camera recording the scene was still able to catch the dancer's smiling face as she flowed around the stage with a lovely grace.

Katelyn angled her hidden view to watch the screen.

"That looks like Janet," Josiah said in frustration. "What was she – in a dance troop in another life?"

As Ethan explained, his face lit up with his quirky smile. "No, this is Janet's mother, Teresa. I wish I could have seen her dance in person. People say that when she danced, they felt transported to heaven. This was recorded about twenty years ago while Janet was just a toddler."

He turned to Josiah and the grin dropped off his face. "Do you know that Teresa lives here on the ranch? She doesn't dance anymore because of a major illness, but she still is an amazing choreographer. That's how I first met the family — while visiting my aunt's workplace in the hospital, where Teresa was recovering from an operation."

As Ethan's words began to draw Josiah away from his anger, Katelyn too relaxed. Her curiosity grew, along with the guilt over her initial response to Josiah's pain. She also shivered with encroaching memories of her mother's illness.

"Janet's father was regularly gone, as he is now with his tenure in the army reserves. This was recorded when he was in the Mideast, preparing for the upcoming conflict before it was public. It was a black ops and Teresa could not be told where he was; if he died on the mission all that she would hear was that he was not coming home, but nothing more. He is currently deployed again over there, somewhere, where it's now even more dangerous for him."

Ethan's tone turned reflective as he moved under the video screen. Watching Teresa dance, he said, "Teresa told me once that she would dance for only two people. One was her husband, whom she felt could sense her love across the miles in every twirl and spin. But, the first person she danced for was the most special gift in her life, Janet. While audiences raved about her performances, Teresa only danced for these two: one who would never see it in person and the other too young to appreciate it."

Josiah's face relaxed, watching the beautiful artistry of Teresa's moves. Katelyn, while drawn into the delight clearly seen in Teresa's expression, wondered with a growing fear what happened to her. Ethan, instead of sharing more on Teresa, moved on.

"Teresa was a very talented dancer but her daughter Janet is extraordinary."

Katelyn focused on the "was" in Ethan's story, and a small moan escaped her lips.

If Ethan heard Katelyn, he didn't acknowledge it, but continued, watching the screen.

"She could easily become a superstar in the ballet world if she wanted to."

"Why doesn't she?" Josiah asked. "What's keeping her in this dead-end hole in the wilderness?"

Katelyn's grip on the French Doors tightened and they shook a little, but neither Ethan nor Josiah acknowledged any movement.

"Janet also only dances for two. She dances for her father, just as her mother did. Every now and then she has the great joy of being able to send him some video clips when he is out of the country. The main person she dances for though is someone who has captured her heart."

"You?" Josiah asked sheepishly, while Ethan paused his story.

Katelyn felt the pause was an eternity. As she waited, fear over Teresa's plight threatened to choke her. It lessened slightly but was replaced with a different fear as she replayed Josiah's question in her mind. Katelyn wanted to run out of the building. Her emotions were seesawing thinking of Teresa, then Janet, and now Ethan. Her breathing fogged up the door glass as she leaned closer with closed eyes, and she thought that surely Josiah and Ethan could hear her heartbeat.

I don't want to hear anymore, she breathed. I don't want to hear anymore. But her legs wouldn't move.

Ethan smiled as the video came to an end. "No," he chuckled. "Janet and I are close friends, but this person loves her with a passion I could never match. "Here, let me show you a clip I recorded this last summer from one of my trips to the ranch."

Hauntingly beautiful worship music filled the room as Josiah and Ethan watched Janet dance on the big screen.

Katelyn forced her eyes open to glimpse Janet's worship, with a beauty and style that surpassed her mother's skill. It echoed what her heart had soared to earlier while worshipping together. Her breathing slowed and her heart settled as she watched Janet express her love through dance.

"When Janet dances you can sense a joy beyond measure as she floats in the air," Ethan said. "If people could see angels when her mother danced, then they would say that Janet actually dances with them."

As Janet came closer to the camera's viewpoint, a rapturous longing shone on her face.

Janet truly looks like one in love, Katelyn thought. I never considered how one's body could be used in such an expression.

Josiah's whole posture relaxed. Ethan stared straight ahead out the windows as the video ended.

He paused as if to leave but turned instead to Josiah and spoke with a sudden sadness.

"There is more to this story."

"Her father hasn't died, has he?" Josiah said, while Katelyn held her breath.

"Concern for someone who has caused you so much trouble, Josiah?" Ethan gently chided.

Josiah looked down at his feet, as Ethan put his hand on his shoulders.

"No, her father is still very much alive, and Janet is trying with all her effort to keep this ranch going for his return."

"You want me to reconsider leaving early and not breaking our contract," Josiah remarked, sitting straight up, and shrugging off Ethan's gesture of friendship.

Ethan looked down. Katelyn could clearly see the disappointment on his face. "Not at all. You need to do what you need to do, Josiah. I just wanted you to see something that I hoped would bless you."

Josiah took a breath and said, "I'm sorry. Some of the advisors have been pressuring me to speak more against this kind of thing. I would describe everything you have shown me with one word: holy. Anything more to the story?"

Katelyn's heart echoed Josiah's request. She wanted to hear more of Janet's mother. She angrily silenced her imagination, as images of her own mother in the hospital demanded attention.

Ethan nodded and continued. "Janet visited our church several times before you came and started your ministry there. One Sunday morning she heard a strange voice in her heart telling her to dance as the worship service was going on. She responded to the voice with a question asking him who he was. The answer she heard back was 'someone who loves you with all his heart.' Janet told me that at that moment her concepts of love underwent a drastic change. She quietly moved out of the pew and went to the back of the auditorium where she started bending and pirouetting with a love that she had never felt before. She told me that she could only breathe one thought back through her closed eyes: that she loved the one who spoke to her with as much fierceness as the power that was capturing her soul."

Katelyn's eyes opened wide, as aching for her new friend washed away her own clamoring memories. She remembered that incident as if it was yesterday. She didn't know the woman was Janet, from being on the other side of the large auditorium that Sunday morning. Katelyn had sought her out after the service but couldn't find her.

Josiah quietly stammered, "What happened next?"

"About halfway through the song, the music minister noticed Janet's actions. He stopped the entire worship service and spoke to her to quit dancing and return to her seat. However, Janet never heard him. She was in a world where angels were singing. When Janet did not respond, the head elder stood up and motioned to the ushers who interrupted her dance, and escorted her out of the auditorium."

Josiah's face reflected the sadness Katelyn was struggling with. Katelyn unsuccessfully held back her tears.

"Janet spent the next several hours crying, but not because of humiliation. She has never told me all the details of that afternoon, but I've pieced together a little. Janet sensed a broken heart as intense as the passion of love that reached into her own soul. She keenly felt a deep grief from heaven over the rejection of a gift that was being offered to everyone."

Josiah glanced at the door. Katelyn shrunk back into the shadows, and knew he was seeing his fiancé rushing out sobbing. As Josiah turned back to Ethan with a chagrined face, she quietly closed to door with just a crack to hear through.

"Janet has never taken up an offense from that day, as far as I can tell," Ethan continued. "And now when you watch her dance you can sense a depth of friendship with her creator that makes me want to know him like she does. She is truly his beloved and he is hers. It awes me to watch her love him through her dance. If you would have been here this afternoon you would have been blessed just to stand in the presence of her affection."

Katelyn didn't need to see Josiah's face to know he was greatly affected by the story. She heard him quietly choke up with emotion and begin to weep. She backed off from the doors with alarm when she heard Ethan walking out of the room.

When Ethan stepped into the foyer the outside front door clicked shut. He glanced at the door with a slightly puzzled expression as he changed shoes, and then lit up with a smile as he sniffed the air. He opened the door and yelled to the fleeing form hurrying down the trail.

"Katelyn, wait up!"

Katelyn slowed and then stopped. She turned a little sheepishly towards Ethan as he caught up to her. "I didn't mean to eavesdrop but you have a way with stories. That was all true, wasn't it?"

"Cross my heart," Ethan motioned.

"It was sad, but beautiful," she said. Katelyn considered asking more about Janet and her mother, but instead, thoughts of her own mother started to engulf her heart.

In the silence of Katelyn's growing blackness, Ethan gently took her hand in his. It jarred Katelyn from the threatening pain.

She didn't object but gave him a sideways glance and said, "Ethan, I do have a boyfriend, and a jealous one at that."

Ethan said nothing and kept holding her hand as they walked back down the bark-covered trail, their breath forming small clouds in the chilled air. Katelyn just enjoyed the quiet and the warm hand, the darkness once again receding.

After a while, Ethan let go as they both had to button up their coats tighter. Katelyn donned some gloves and Ethan put his hands in his coat pockets. The increasing cold froze the air around them into greater stillness, till the crunch of their boots on the trail made them both want to slow down to match the silence of the forest.

"You're on the youth group leadership council, right?" Ethan said. "It looks like you are in for another challenging and late evening."

"I don't see a need to bring up Janet's past if that is worrying you," Katelyn said.

"No. I know you and Janet have started a special friendship. I was just worried about you. Don't doze off at the table," he smiled.

Ethan's words seem to accentuate the sudden loss of Katelyn's energy from the sleepless night and day's activities. A great weariness began inching its way up her legs with every step.

They continued to the main lodge in silence. Somehow, through all the turmoil surfacing this weekend, the man at her side extended a confidence that everything would work out. Her exhaustion, however, began clouding the hope he offered, and she wondered if the coming snow storm signaled a greater approaching darkness.

11. Awakening

Katelyn started worrying in her dream about what Ethan was going to do next, as his odd smile appeared in front of her. Worrying became shock when she realized her eyes were open, and it was no dream.

Pale orange moonlight from the gibbous moon pierced the thick storm clouds racing across the skies, leaked through the thin curtains behind her, and dimly lit up Ethan's face. He was propped up on one elbow staring at Katelyn from across the bed. She could read the amused look on his face even through the shadows. Ethan remained still as her eyes opened wider in alarm.

Before she could speak her escalating emotions, he whispered to her, "You are lovely in the morning."

Katelyn discarded her drowsiness immediately for complete alertness, followed by anger. She took a deep breath as strong words began to form. Ethan readied to leave the bed but stopped as he watched Katelyn's reaction. He reached his free hand out from under the patchwork comforter and brought his finger almost to Katelyn's lips.

"Careful," he quietly warned. "The walls are paper thin."

Ethan did not move his hand until Katelyn slowly scooted backwards to the edge of the bed, pulling the comforter up to her chin. As she did, she recognized that she still had her clothes on from the day before, except her boots. It did not quell her feelings. She grasped the blanket tighter and edged herself out of the bed onto the cold floor, not taking her eyes off of Ethan, dragging the bedspread with her. Wrapping the warm blanket around herself she took several more steps backward, not taking her eyes off this insane interloper. The past days with this man were utterly forgotten as the anger in her heart rose in waves, flushing her face with heat. She released the huge breath building inside of her and whispered a screaming retort, "What are you doing here? Where is Natalie?"

"I am sure that Natalie is asleep in her bed, probably shivering because you are not there to keep her warm," he said softly. "I might ask instead what you are doing in my room – in my bed?"

Ethan's reply caused Katelyn to gasp as she heard the honesty in his question. She quickly looked around. The details were subtle, but even in the greyness she realized this was not the room she shared with Natalie. Her anger streaked away as quickly as it had erupted but the redness in her face rose to crimson. She blushed to her toes and hoped that Ethan could not see her burning cheeks.

"I...I thought this was my room," Katelyn stammered, her emotions whipsawing back and forth between confusion and relief. "I fell asleep in front of the fire last night after the leader's meeting. I hardly remember climbing the stairs and crawling into bed. I was so exhausted. The flashlight went out. I thought this was my room," she repeated, her voice becoming smaller and more desperate.

"You could have been a train whistling through the room and you wouldn't have woken me up," Ethan said. "Aunt D says the only way she can get me up when I am dead to the world is to bring a pan of sizzling bacon right under my nose. I think that's what woke me up; the smell of your perfume. Though how I can smell it through the odor of what I used on my hair last night, I'll never know. That will teach me to use someone's shampoo."

Ethan's grin widened to the farthest edge of his mouth as he observed the many thoughts flickering across Katelyn's gaze. "Not to say that your perfume smells like bacon. It smells beautiful – just like you."

Katelyn's eyes hardened. "Will you stop that?"

"Please," Katelyn whispered as Ethan did not answer, though she wasn't sure if her plea referred to his words, his silent stare, or the stirring of a strange feeling fanning out from her heart.

Katelyn tried to focus her gaze, but the soft reflections in the room barely lit Ethan's face, blurring his eyes into a single dark pool. Feeling drawn into their depths, panic again surfaced in Katelyn's mind, overwhelming the quiet song that was beginning to arise in her heart.

She said the first words that came to mind.

"What you told me yesterday about being captivated – you're just infatuated."

She watched a flicker of sadness interrupt the joy that bathed Ethan's face and suddenly felt ashamed. Ethan quickly recovered and smiled back at her with furrowed brows.

"Did I tell you how lovely you are in the morning?"

Tears welled up in Katelyn's eyes. Without moving her focus from Ethan's gaze, she slightly relaxed her tense grip on the blankets, inched back slowly to sit on the bed, and released words from some deep place of fractured hope.

"I'm sorry," she said. "This looks like all my fault."

"Looks?"

"Something is happening here. I feel everything around me changing. My stumbling into the wrong room almost seems like no accident. Ethan, what is going on? What are you doing to me?"

"Me?"

"I've cried more in front of you than anybody I can remember. How can the world unravel in a few days?"

"Unravel?"

"It is like something bottled up inside me wants out. But if I let it go, it will swallow up everything I have ever known. Ethan, I feel a longing for something I can't explain," she sighed.

Katelyn noticed Ethan's quick intake of breath and suddenly became afraid. Please God. Don't let him think this longing is for him.

Ethan released his view of Katelyn and looked past her toward the window, where the moonlight was gradually being covered by new storm clouds. He slowly raised himself off his bent arm and sat up.

He gazed through the thin window curtain, barely covering the glass pane. Katelyn could see that he was looking beyond the hills and setting moon, to something beyond the distant mountains. His words pierced Katelyn to her core. "A far green country."

Katelyn blinked, sending tears down her cheeks. Hope knocked on the cage walls of her heart. Thoughts of a growing mystery began to intrude upon her pain, filling her with wonder.

She saw that Ethan's sight was still riveted beyond the window as he repeated quietly, "You long for a far green country. I know. I too yearn for that place. Tolkien penned those words to describe a land beyond this life – a heaven if you like. I see it as something greater. It is a place where love is always shared in truth and the barriers to our hearts can be released with a thought. A place where 'goodbyes' are never sorrowful because you are always close to everyone you love, beyond the pablum spoken to you that a loved one will always be with you."

Katelyn quieted as his words salved her troubled thoughts.

He continued, returning his stare to Katelyn with a gentle look. "It is the home you have always wished for. Beauty is its air and you breathe it with every hope."

Riddles danced in Katelyn's spirit. Snow began to fall again, and the room began to grow darker as the moon became obscured by a curtain of white. She felt peace flowing with the growing shadows and filling every corner with its warmth, like a fire in the hearth on Christmas Eve. Katelyn turned her eyes toward the window, expecting a glow from some distant land to light up the night.

Ethan moved finally and gently inched himself off the bed. He padded to his duffle and rummaged by feel for his clothes. Katelyn kept her view on the window as she listened to Ethan dressing. She clutched the bedspread tighter to herself as the chill of the evening returned. Ethan's boots scraped against the floor as he picked them up and glided like a shadow towards the door.

"Ethan," she sighed to the dark figure heading out of the room. She heard a hand grasp the handle, begin to crack open the door, and then stop. "A far green country. I want to live there. How do you get such faith?" she whispered.

The sliver of light gray that appeared at the open door faded as Ethan closed the door. She felt more than saw his presence ease back towards her, until their view was only filled with each other's shimmering eyes. Katelyn marveled at her calm as Ethan's face filled her world. He leaned towards her and kissed away a tear on her cheeks. Backing up, he once again became a silent shadow.

He seems like a man who has found out how to live in the silence, Katelyn wondered. Or is it just simple peace?

Ethan whispered to her finally in the stillness. "It is also a land where there is no shame in desire because truth shines from every heart. Passion reigns for there is no fear. And, it is so much more than just a place."

Katelyn could almost hear the grin spread across Ethan's face in the darkness as he spoke his joy. The silence stretched for several seconds and then Ethan padded softly towards the door.

Before turning the handle, he looked back and quietly spoke, "When you said I was infatuated with you, you were partly right. I am *utterly* infatuated with you, Katelyn Braselli."

The craziness of his words stirred her frustration again. "What does 'utterly infatuated' mean, Ethan McGregor? And, don't you dare give me any more mysterious explanations."

"Ask Natalie. She knows."

"Ethan!" she screamed in a high whisper.

But Ethan had already turned and was twisting the doorknob. Before cracking open the door Katelyn heard a low voice breathing from his shadow. "You might not know it my phantom of the night but you are lovely in the morning."

He then quickly opened the door wide enough to ease himself out into the black hallway, and shut it without a sound. As the door closed Katelyn shook her head at the ridiculous circumstances and riddles. She reached her hand up to her cheek where a young man's kiss had given her the strangest mystery of all, and then smiled into the darkness as a tendril of peace reached its way into her heart.

12. Mountain Crest

"You never came to bed?" Natalie asked. "You look well-rested for someone who probably slept on a chair."

Natalie had just sat down next to Katelyn in the foyer; taking a break from helping to prepare breakfast. She handed Katelyn a mug of tea and said, "I found some blackberry, your favorite. Careful — hot."

"I did come to bed," Katelyn said, taking a sip. "It's an interesting story," she finished to Natalie's raised eyebrows. The fruity vapors rose from the tea, but she could still smell the essential oils on Natalie's hair. She smiled at the memory of that fragrance from last night's strange encounter.

"Really? This sounds interesting, since I didn't hear or feel you all night. When I got up early, I wondered why the huge comforter I put between us didn't move."

"I'll tell you all of it, I promise, but I need to ask you a question first."

"Alright," Natalie smiled. "This sounds a little dramatic."

Natalie scooted her chair a little closer. They were sitting in an alcove off the foyer, way to the side of the fireplace, where others of the youth group had circled and were planning their fun day in the snow, trapped at the lodge – all angst from the youth advisors forgotten.

Natalie touched a forefinger from each hand to her eyes, then pointed both towards Katelyn. It was their secret sign meaning all eyes on you.

Katelyn got up and scooted her large overstuffed chair even closer, until their legs gently touched.

"Nat," Katelyn began. "The boy who's been hounding you – Nick."

Natalie released a breath.

"Phew – this seems innocent enough. You had me worried there for a while. Well, I wouldn't say hounding, exactly. More like following me around with a lost puppy-dog face. Kind of cute really. Yesterday, he…"

"Nat. Focus." Katelyn interrupted. "I need to understand something here."

"OK, but Kat, what's Nick got to do with anything?"

"If he told you that he was way beyond infatuated with you, how would you describe his feelings?"

"Way beyond infatuated? What do you mean?"

"He came up to you, took your hands in his, and told you with all the seriousness he could put into words, that he was *utterly* infatuated with you. What would that mean to you?"

Natalie's eyes grew wide and she looked off into the fireplace before answering. Seconds went by and Natalie still did not answer.

"Hello Nat. You still there?" Katelyn asked, putting a hand on Natalie's knee.

Natalie turned, sighed, and finally answered, "Well, I would say that he probably *thought* that he was in love with me."

Both girls trembled with Natalie's answer. Memories swirled in Katelyn's mind. She replayed the picture of Ethan speaking to her from the doorway. The beauty of the conversation surrounding a land of love and peace echoed its stillness in her heart. But then Katelyn gasped.

The joy of that conversation was interrupted by a truth that had been staring at her for some time now. Ethan had given her another riddle in his answer, and it threatened to throw her over a cliff.

"Natalie," Katelyn began, using her full name for the first in a long time. Natalie took a breath and held it as Katelyn's gaze pierced her eyes.

"Really?" Katelyn quietly breathed.

Tears began to pool in Natalie's eyes, but she didn't say anything.

Images were flashing through Katelyn's memory of the last several years. Words, gentle tilts of the head during their frequent times together, and late-night discussions where Natalie gave Katelyn amazing insights on reacting to her boyfriend's moods played through her mind. Slight motions that only now had meaning bubbled to the surface, ending with the way Natalie and Ben behaved when she came upon them praying. Truth, stark and bare, framed itself in one word.

"Benjamin?" Katelyn whispered.

"Oh – Katelyn," Natalie sobbed. Natalie reached out and took her best friend's hands as Katelyn turned away. Natalie reached up with one hand and gently moved Katelyn's face so that both could see each other's water-clouded eyes.

"You are my best, bestest, and forever bestest friend," Natalie said. "I never wanted...I don't know how it happened. One day, I woke up and realized...I am so sorry. Oh – Kat."

Another riddle answered itself to Katelyn, watching Natalie confess her breaking heart.

"You have never told him how much you care for him."

"Of course not! I could never do that to you."

"All those years, listening to my late-night teenager whining over her boyfriend, hanging out with us. Sitting beside him, watching him fawn over me. Hiding your feelings all that time – for me?" Katelyn asked with wonder.

"Kat – I love you. There was never any other path," Natalie wept.

"Nat – you are a friend beyond friends."

"You don't hate me?"

"Oh – never!"

Katelyn reached over and both girls cried into each other's shoulders. They pulled back after a moment, wiping the tears off each other's faces.

Katelyn took Natalie's face into her hands and said, "Janet gave us clues and Ethan revealed the mystery. We have learned well how to lie to everyone around us, and wear a mask. We think we are serving everybody but the lies surrounding us are proof that we are trying to simply hide our pain. And the worst is that our entire life becomes a lie, burying love and all its joy — destroying the friendships that are so precious."

Katelyn watched Natalie's eyes open wide at hearing her confirm the value of their friendship. With a smile, she sealed away forever any thought that might challenge the love between them.

"So, what are we going to do now?" Natalie asked.

"I'm not sure, but let's take today as it comes, and promise something to each other," Katelyn said.

"What?"

"To let love prosper."

Both girls grinned at each other and embraced. As they were hugging, Ethan and Ben walked into the room, their heads swinging around looking for something. They spotted the girls in the corner and quickly walked over. As they got closer, they saw Natalie and Katelyn smiling through tears and embracing. They both just stood there for a while glancing at each other, with a shared look asking that the other person start the conversation.

"What?" Katelyn and Natalie asked in unison.

Ethan answered, "Janet is looking for you, Katelyn. It's important."

The girls just glared at them. Ben grabbed Ethan's arm and dragged Ethan from the room as if he suddenly remembered an emergency. The girls laughed and hugged again.

"Kat," Natalie started with some more hesitation as they relaxed back in their chairs.

"More, best friend?"

Natalie slightly tensed again and continued. "Yesterday when I finally dragged your Ben/West Point conversation out of you, I..."

"It's Ok, Nat. I know what you are about to confess. You already knew Ben was going to West Point. I may be half blind about what's happening in front of me, but I am still good at evaluating the past. I do want to know something, though. Did you start looking for a college to transfer to in New York before or after you found out Ben was trying to get into the Academy? Don't go sheepish on me," she said, watching Natalie drop her gaze to the floor.

"After. Ben never volunteered his plans to me, Kat, – really," she answered. "I just figured it out from hints he was dropping and asked him one day while we were waiting for you after class. He made me promise not to tell you. The big lunk said he was going to come clean with you right away. That was months ago – I've been on his case ever since."

"Nat," Katelyn said grabbing Natalie's hands this time. "I have been in my own world for a while and feel like I am just starting to wake up. Do you mind one last question?"

"Course not – go ahead."

"Tell me about your prayer with Ben the other night. Not the facts; Ben told me what you were praying about. What happened between you two? I can hardly ever get Ben to pray with me. I clearly saw – something."

More tears started to well up in Natalie's eyes as she stammered out the last piece of truth.

Natalie took a deep breath and said, "You know me. I can't pray without holding hands so I grabbed

Ben's big paws. It all happened so fast, and then we were both praying." Natalie lowered her voice and spoke more gently. "It was like a door opened into our hearts as we prayed. I opened my eyes and there were his – looking straight into my soul. He kind of looked shocked. I am sure he saw the depths of feeling I had for him. And then I saw something."

Natalie stopped, looking afraid again, but Katelyn gave her an almost imperceptible nod. "Go on Nat," Katelyn said softly.

The final pieces of the puzzle of Ben's relationship had already clicked into place in Katelyn's mind. Surprisingly, Katelyn had no more tears. Where a hollow spot should have been in her heart, ready to be filled with anger, vengeance, and sorrow was instead a calm, clear lake. The riddle of a "far green country" wafted over her thoughts, filling her with the strangest peace she ever felt.

Natalie continued, reliving the wonder of the moment. "I saw his heart, too, clear as anything I have ever seen. And what I saw. Well, this time – I was shocked."

It was Katelyn's turn to grasp Natalie's hands, now feeling her trying to pull away.

"Kat, I never meant for any of this to happen," Natalie moaned.

"Of course not, Nat. You are, and will always be my dearest friend," and then they were hugging again.

"Kat, what is bringing all this stuff with everybody to a head?" Natalie wondered out loud, as she wiped tears off her face with the back of her hand. "It's like we all signed up to attend an inner healing spa, except with horse dung and a blizzard."

Katelyn laughed, surprising herself. "Nat – you always have a way with words. Not sure, but there is one new, common variable in this place."

"Ethan," they both said in unison.

"So, what's going on with you and him?" Natalie hesitantly asked.

"Oh, nothing serious," Katelyn quickly flipped back. "He just told me early this morning that he was utterly infatuated with me as he left the bedroom."

13. Passions

Natalie's eyes opened wider than her mouth.

Just as Katelyn settled back and took a breath, Janet hurriedly entered the room. She looked around, and seeing the girls, rushed over.

"Plans changed," she said to Katelyn. "Just your dad is taking you. Hurry, you need to leave as soon as you can."

"What plans?" Katelyn asked, being raised up by Janet's strong grip.

"Ethan and Ben didn't tell you? By that look on your face – obviously not. The Double Bar Ranch is a smaller sister ranch to ours west of here. They got hit with the storm worse than us yesterday and are still digging out. They are having some serious problems with a couple of horses. Worse, all their crew is stuck in Idaho with the pass still being closed, and they can't get any veterinarian help. You are up."

"Me? I can't!"

"Yes, you can. I have the utmost confidence in you. And Natalie, what's wrong?" Janet spat at her. "You look like you just swallowed a peach pit."

"Nothing," Natalie gargled.

"Come with me quick," Janet pulled Katelyn. "I'll give you more details and some supplies as you get your coat. We need to hurry, not just for the horses, but before the weather turns more miserable."

Katelyn looked back as she was dragged out of the room. Natalie appeared to be strangling with frustration. Finding a well of courage she didn't know she had, Katelyn mouthed to her, "Ask Ethan," and then disappeared around the corner.

Grabbing her winter coat and some boots, Katelyn followed Janet to a side storage room with a locked cupboard. Janet unlocked the door, quickly emptied some paper out of a box, gave it to Katelyn to hold, and started filling it with animal medical supplies. Fear gripped Katelyn's mind as she saw Janet throw in syringes, drugs, antiseptic, and bandages.

"Janet, I can't do this," she stuttered.

"Didn't you help Dr. Wilde yesterday, giving shots?" Janet asked as she continued to fill up the box.

"Well sure, but that was different."

"Not to a horse it isn't. Look," Janet said, stopping and grasping Katelyn's shoulders. "I might be able to help, but there is no way I can be gone today. You are the only hope some recently caught wild mustangs have. You are smart and know how to take charge – so take charge."

Janet then pulled a couple of worn books off the shelf next to the supplies. "Here," she said throwing them into the box. "These might help."

Katelyn followed Janet to the kitchen carrying the box of supplies. Janet grabbed some food and drinks, then headed back to the main entrance out into the parking lot with Katelyn in tow. A small path had been shoveled in the sidewalk up to a large black Ford pickup. The feet of snow that had fallen last night was whisked off the top of the truck, filling most of the back bed, but the falling snow had already put a layer of white back on the truck.

Janet opened the back quad-door cab and Katelyn loaded the supplies and food. She glanced over the seat and saw her dad already at the wheel warming up the truck. As she was about to get in, she caught Ethan and Ben trudging through the snow, manhandling a bale of the artificial test bed hay. They stomped up to the truck, and as Janet let down the rear tailgate, they threw the hay in. The truck made a noticeable lurch with the new weight. Katelyn stepped up into the idling truck facing a blast of hot air from the heater vent.

Janet closed the tailgate, waved bye, and headed in. Ethan walked over to the driver's side through the snow, while Ben headed up to Katelyn's side. She heard Ethan tell her father that they were good to go with the added weight in the back while Ben motioned for Katelyn to lower her window. Katelyn lowered it half way to keep the snow already on the window from falling into her lap.

"Be safe," Ben said.

Katelyn spoke through the opening, "When I get back, we need to talk some more. Ok?"

Ben just nodded, a slightly worried frown painting his face.

"It is going to be alright, Ben," she said with a smile. "Just keep the fireplace going."

Ethan had trudged around to Katelyn's side and managed to get in a "You can do it!" with a face full of smiles, before she raised her window and he was obscured by the melting snow.

Braz checked that the truck was in four-wheel drive mode and then eased out of the parking lot. The off-road mud tires easily chewed through the fresh snow and he slowly pulled onto the main entrance road. He loosened his tight grip on the steering wheel as the truck displayed its stability on the slick snow-covered surface.

The main drive curved through pine tree borders for several miles and at the farthest end met up with a small river running parallel to the road. The river ditch was wide and deep, filled with snow, with a small stream visible through the snow drifts. As he crossed a bridge, where the river ran under the road, the driveway ended and Braz turned off onto Highway 37 heading west. The road appeared to have had a snowplow go by in the last couple of hours, since only several inches of snow coated its surface. A half-buried 80 mph sign was slightly visible through the continuing curtain of white. Braz's grip on the steering wheel relaxed as he sped up to a comfortable 35 mph, clods of ice and powder flying from the rear tires.

"You look a little freaked," Braz said to his daughter.

"You think? Great observation powers, Dad."

"Look, just because I say never let them see you sweat doesn't mean that arguing a case in front of a judge, jury, and prosecutor is a cakewalk. I know how you feel."

"Dad, you are never nervous arguing a case."

"Well, that's true," he smiled back at her. "I just thought it would be a great anecdote."

Katelyn just shook her head at her father's poor attempt at humor and peered through the slowly swiping windshield washers into the gray gloom of falling snow.

"Whose truck is this, and what did Janet mean about you kicking Ethan and Ben out?" Katelyn asked.

"This is Ethan's truck and I didn't kick him or Ben out. Both of them, and probably Natalie, were going to take you, but then I intruded and said that I wanted to come. Ethan changed his mind and recommended that this might be a good time for us to catch up on things, alone – whatever that means. Ben bowed out right quick after, and I don't think they ever got around to inviting Natalie. Alright with just your dad?"

"Of course," she answered. "How long till we get there?"

"The directions are pretty simple, and would normally take around 30 minutes, but I wouldn't bet on less than two hours with this weather."

The big questions were answered so Katelyn relaxed in her seat. She glanced around the truck to get a feel about Ethan from the interior but all she could read was that he was neat; the truck was clean, without any of the normal detritus that accompanied pickup owners. Katelyn wished that the large number of thoughts and issues rolling about in her mind could be likewise tidied up into something neat.

"Dad, I do need to talk to you, and maybe this will be a good time for that, but I have to do something first," Katelyn said. "I need to study up on some of these books Janet gave me. I can't let these horses…"

"– and people," her dad interjected.

"– down," Katelyn finished with a smile.

She gave her dad's arm a squeeze and reached back for the manuals Janet had thrown in the box. Katelyn settled into the large comfortable seat and buried her head in the treatment and care of horses, while her dad quietly drove. Several hours passed by without conversation or incident, and she finally looked up, feeling the truck slow and turn. It passed under a snow-covered bare pine pole entryway, with the carved sign of a script "D" above two solid lines on the top sign.

They pulled up the circle driveway, its edges marked by the tops of reflector poles in the deep snow, and stopped in front of a single floor timber and rock building. It looked idyllic as a postcard with the recent snowfall. As Braz shut off the engine, a large burly man, with a beard to match his girth, lurched out of the front door. He had no coat, only a stained brown shirt flopping out over his large belly, half tucked into filthy and wet work jeans.

"Are you from Singing Hills?" he wheezed with excitement to Katelyn as she stepped out of the truck.

"Yes," Katelyn said, surprised at the confidence in her voice and the relief on the man's face.

"Thank God!" the man replied, without acknowledging Braz. "I'm Franz. Hurry, please. Follow me."

Braz trailed the two, carrying the box of medical supplies. Katelyn glanced back and saw the amusement on his face. Katelyn would have normally responded with a funny quip about Dad being a porter, but her mind was already filled with remedies for sick horses.

Katelyn and Braz followed Franz along a thin worn path in the snow around the office building to the stables. Franz explained to Katelyn how there happened to be only a few hands at the ranch when the storm hit. The owner and his family, along with the foreman and horse wrangler, were driving back from a conference in Seattle, but were held up when the pass closed.

This was a much smaller spread than the Singing Hill ranch; still it contained a good size modern stable. More than a foot of snow covered the steep stable roof while six-foot drifts were piled up on the windward side. Franz opened the stable door against a pile of snow, which could only open enough to allow Braz to sidestep in with the box, and quickly pointed out the several horses to Katelyn. He then made a quick cell phone call back to Janet to let her know that they had arrived.

Katelyn faced a moment of panic as she heard several wild mustangs neighing in distress, saw a chestnut mare coughing and wheezing, and smelled the odor of soiled bedding. A tired looking young teenager approached them from an end stall and began answering Katelyn's questions.

Katelyn quickly took charge, banishing the feelings that threatened to root her to the spot. She put on gloves and approached the first suffering animal. She identified symptoms of equine influenza and put on a mask while talking softly to the struggling horse. Katelyn tried to contain her anger at the apparent fungus and ringworm that was evident on several of the other horses – diseases that would not appear suddenly like the flu but were indications of poor horse care.

She asked for hot water, and then directed the two hands to bring the bale of hay out of the back of the pickup truck. Showing her father how to prepare some poultices, she began to examine the worst horses, giving a shot where needed.

"Katelyn," her father said. "Ethan and Ben loaded that hay in the truck for added weight. How can it help the horses?"

"It is a special artificial hay, Dad," she answered. "It is formulated to repel moisture, and right now these horses need some additional bedding. The ride here in the snow will not have soaked the hay like most of what I see piled up here."

She pointed the ranch hands to the stalls that needed to be cleaned out and showed them how to bank the special hay.

"Do you happen to have a home vaporizer anywhere?" she asked Franz.

"I think there is one in the office," he answered and ran off to get it.

When he returned, Katelyn fashioned it, along with a feeding trough and horse blanket, into a makeshift nebulizer for the worst mustang, who could hardly breathe through its coughs and bloody nose. She worked without pause for several hours, and finally inspected the remaining healthy horses. She gave some a small booster shot, and then followed back giving final comforting talks to the sick animals, while checking the temporary bandages. The horse that had been breathing the antiseptic mist from the vaporizer was breathing much easier.

The young ranch hand and Franz were all smiles with Katelyn's care, and couldn't stop thanking them with handshakes as they left the barn.

14. Heart String

Katelyn tidied up and wrote down further instructions for the ranch hands until the vet or owner arrived. Before heading out, Braz pulled a piece of paper out of his pocket and coerced Franz with a stern look to sign, relieving Katelyn from any liability for the care of the horses. Katelyn gave her dad a look as he pocketed the signed document.

"Never leave home without an indemnification form," he winked. "Great job there, girl. You were awesome."

They both climbed into the truck. Braz started the vehicle, set the heat on high, and began driving back to the highway. Katelyn gave one last wave to the ranch hands and settled back in her seat with a sigh. The adrenaline of the last several hours seeped out of Katelyn's veins and she became drowsy and nodded. She awoke with a jerk after thirty minutes and wondered where she was and why Ethan's face wasn't looking down at her.

"Hi sleepy-head," her father said. "Feeling better? Here is a Coke that Janet packed if that sounds good."

The cold soda sparked Katelyn fully awake and she sat up and took a deep breath.

"I really meant it when I said job well done," Braz said to his daughter. "You made your dear old dad really proud."

"Thanks," she said.

After a moment's silence Katelyn spoke to her father without trying to organize her thoughts. "Dad, I need to share something with you. I woke up last night in Ethan's bed."

Braz's foot hit the brake and the truck skidded to a halt, fortunately alone on the snow-covered highway. He looked over at her with a serious look, but he remained silent. Katelyn, too, stayed quiet, allowing her father to start riddling out the scene with his brilliant mind.

"I was just starting to like that guy," her father replied with an intensity Katelyn was very familiar with. "Wait, you said woke up." Braz squinted at her. "You didn't say slept." His eyebrows lifted and Katelyn knew that was the sign for more details.

"Sorry, Dad," she said, relaxing against the seatbelt. "I didn't mean to shock you. It was all real innocent, I assure you – nothing happened," she continued. Her father's face remained questioning.

He put the truck back in gear and started off, still silent, but Katelyn could see the smoldering behind his eyes.

"You tucked me into the large comforter on the couch in front of the fireplace, after the leadership meeting finished," Katelyn said. "I meant to head right to bed but my eyelids were so heavy. I think I was asleep before you left the room."

Katelyn was staring straight ahead at the falling snow with a wistful expression as her memory replayed the moments.

"I woke up about an hour later and started up the stairs when my flashlight went out. I thought I had climbed to the third floor but obviously not. The halls were dark but I felt for the number "6" on the door and entered what I thought was my room. I smelled Nat's new special shampoo mixture on who I thought was obviously her and just crawled under the covers. I think I did manage to take off my shoes. I woke up near morning with Ethan peering down at me. He left the room a couple of minutes later, Dad. Nothing happened."

Katelyn watched her father's face. He finally took a deep breath and sighed, then eased his grip on the steering wheel.

"Something *did* happen Katelyn, but go on," he said. I know you're not telling me this because you feel guilty."

Katelyn smiled back with love and continued. "I snuck out of the room right after and slinked up the stairs back to my room in the dark. By the way, Ethan's room number is the same as Nat's and mine."

"Did he kiss you?" Braz asked.

"Dad!" Katelyn responded.

"I know the answer to that one already. He told me that he thought he might get the opportunity. So – we have a funny little Reader's Digest moment, that might make a good short story someday," Braz said. "But that's not what's behind this talk, is it?"

Katelyn paused, always amazed at her dad's keen insight. "No," she said. She leaned back into the seat corner and peered through the swishing windshield wipers.

"I need to ask you a question, Dad. Darkness has floated to the surface, and I think with Ethan's help it has started to lose its grip on me. It's about mom."

Braz didn't reply at first, but Katelyn could see the rising tension as Braz stiffened in the seat. "Katelyn," he said. "I really don't…"

"Dad," she interrupted. "Do you hate God for not healing mom?"

The only sound for several minutes was the loud crunch of the tires through the packed snow and the windshield wipers keeping time with the purring engine. Finally, Braz answered.

"We did everything we could, as you well know. Doctors. Cutting edge treatments. And the same on the spiritual side. Twenty-four-seven prayer vigils. Special intercession meetings. Fasting. A group of women that came and spoke nothing but positive stuff round the clock. They carted your mom to several of the healing rooms around the area. She was identified on national prayer lists. The amount of people invested in obtaining God's healing was truly amazing," Braz slowly finished.

Katelyn was stirred by her father's words, knowing this is as difficult for him as it is for her.

"I struggled watching your mom deteriorate. Her death was almost a relief, until I started asking the hard questions. I got no answers, at least none that I could understand, so yes, my feelings towards God got pretty low."

Braz was gripping and releasing the steering wheel as he relived the circumstances of his wife's illness. "I buried my anger – for you. It was always there, though, like a goat head in my running shoes, eating away at my belief in God. Something happened about a year ago that started the healing. I never shared this with you, but it has come to mean a great deal to me, and now seems the right time."

"Go on," Katelyn said with wide-eyed interest.

"Remember when I was in the middle of the Barnard case and I came down with that severe case of pneumonia? You know how bad it got since it was you who had to drag me to the hospital. After several days of not getting much better I became a terrible patient," he said with slight regret.

"Oh really – tell me something I don't know," Katelyn said with a grin, glad for a story that eased the tension of her memories.

"It wasn't just the physical hassles, but the trial had to be postponed and key witnesses became unavailable. Somehow, I blamed God for that whole mess, and then all the pain surfaced for what happened or did not happen with your mom. I was angry at everybody. The people who I ended up venting on were the ones trying to get me better – the nurses. I never told you, because I was ashamed, but I sent several nurses crying from my room with my horrible behavior."

Katelyn watched her father with love as he confessed his weakness. She unbuckled her seatbelt, lifted up the center armrest console, and moved to the center seat. She placed her hands on his arms as he drove.

"Well, this head nurse walks in," he continued. "I'm expecting a real chewing out – for which I was more than ready to engage in. Instead, she just quietly checked all the tubes going in me, then pulled up a chair next to the bed, and gently laid her hand on my shoulder. With a sincerity that I knew was real, she just asked me how I was feeling. No rebuke. No arguing. Just...compassion. I was totally disarmed and mumbled that I was fine. She knew I was not sharing the truth but didn't judge me at all. She simply said, with a gentle look, 'We are going to help you get better.'"

"It was the kindest thing I had felt in a very long time. When she left the room, it seemed that she took all my anger with her. She looked back as she closed the door and just gave me a tender smile."

Braz sighed with the memory.

"I was discharged in a couple of days but came back later and gave all the nurses who had treated me an apology, chocolate, and some tickets to an upcoming Celtic Women concert. I didn't see the head nurse when I returned, so I never got to thank her personally. I did write a letter to Administration thanking them for her care."

"So that's what the tickets were for," Katelyn said as she moved closer. "I found out that you had bought them and was a little bothered that you did not get me one."

"I can't explain it," Braz said. Katelyn laid her head on her father's shoulder as she heard the awe in his voice.

"The pain and anger over what happened to your mom started to fade from that day in the hospital, being replaced by a growing seed of trust. I need to apologize to you too, Katelyn," her dad said. "You always seemed so strong, yet we needed to have this conversation for a long time. I always found an excuse to delay it."

"I buried my feelings, Dad. I don't think until this weekend, I would have been ready to face them. Instead of anger I stopped believing God was good – that he listened. I never heard any answers either, so my relationship with him got put on a shelf. If he wouldn't talk then neither would I. I have just begun to see that my choice started affecting a lot of things."

"Ben, sweetheart?" Braz asked. Katelyn didn't say anything but Braz nodded as a sad look came over her face. "And then Ethan comes along."

"Yes, Ethan," Katelyn sighed. "In just one weekend he stirs up more stuff than a sandstorm."

"Besides your mom, what else has he stirred up in you, pumpkin?" Braz softly asked his daughter.

Katelyn remained quiet for a moment, trying to put her feelings into words.

"He didn't say much as I was wrestling with finding myself in his bed. The simple things he said were riddles I have never thought of. The mysteries he shared have kind of faded, but they planted something in me I have not felt for a long time – hope."

Katelyn stayed silent for several moments then smiled. The memory of the light of truth during the worship dance floated across her mind again, but the more she reached for it the more it flew out of mind. Almost forgetting she was talking to her father, Katelyn continued.

"He spoke to me with more than just his words. I saw a passion in his eyes so deep that I thought I might drown. His feelings were not about consuming me or using me. There was simply a depth of desire only for me that I have never experienced, even during all the years with Ben."

Braz completed Katelyn's thought. "He would do anything, go anywhere, and pay any price to rescue you, wouldn't he?"

"Yes!" Katelyn blushed at her father's understanding of the intimacy she had experienced. "I immediately felt small, but his gaze was like a huge net – pulling me away from a focus on myself, and not letting me go until I understood how much I meant to him. It was terrifying, and yet at the same time, wonderful."

Katelyn could feel her father relax and quieted, lost in her thoughts. There were whispers in the deepest part of Katelyn's heart that the affection from Ethan was part of something bigger; a picture of a caring heart from someone who had never stopped reaching out to her regardless of her retreat into doubt.

They continued the ride without any further conversation, with Katelyn still snuggled up against her father. They were almost at the ranch turnoff when Braz broke the silence with a question. "Would you mind, daughter, if your dad started seeing someone?"

Katelyn moved back against her side door and looked at her dad with surprise. "A woman?"

Braz again gave her a look of raised eyebrows. "Seriously, Katelyn. This may come as a little shock to you but I too have received a gift this weekend. I guess you would call it a slice of humility; the possibility that my judgments are only seeing a part of the truth. And, I have been remembering that head nurse at the hospital. I don't recall if she was married and maybe she no longer works there but I would like to find out. I keep smiling every time I remember her pretty face and gentle kindness. What do you think?"

Katelyn was seriously impressed by her dad's revelation, but still couldn't resist jabbing him back. "Pretty face?" she smiled.

"Yes," her dad grinned into the windshield, oblivious to Katelyn's ribbing. "She was very fair – not tan at all, but it suited her well. Light flawless skin, a little like Ethan's."

Katelyn considered a peculiar thought. "Dad, do you remember her name?"

"Oh yes. That I remember. It was a lovely name. Desirée."

Katelyn started laughing and couldn't stop.

"What?" her dad asked, slightly irritated. He had just exited slowly off the highway towards the ranch, while Katelyn continued to laugh, now almost uncontrollably. Braz followed the curving road, crossing the small bridge over the river. He was scowling as he turned the truck down the long entrance-way to the ranch, which had gained over six inches of snow since they had left that morning.

"Do you know who that is?" she chortled.

"No, but I bet you can't wait to tell me." Braz locked his eyes on Katelyn with a dangerous glare. "And buckle your seatbelt."

"She is…" Katelyn started but never got to finish. The truck suddenly spun totally around, skidded off the road into the steep crevasse edging the river, and began flipping sideways. Her world turned into screams, broken glass, and then just the silence of falling snow.

15. Music

Katelyn awoke to a splitting headache and uncontrollable shivering. The trembling in her limbs quickly became pain as her mind finally broke through its fog to connect with her body.

She was lying in ice water on her back, on the inside of the truck passenger door. Her head was cradled in what looked like a white plastic sheet; the remains of the side air bag. Her back barely felt the sharp gravel and broken glass that she lay in because of the near-freezing water swirling around her crumpled form, and she couldn't feel her feet at all. It dawned on her as the humming in her ears lessened that the truck was laying on its side, apparently in the river bed.

Above her was her father, unconscious and suspended by his seatbelt.

"Dad!" she screamed, but she was only answered by a moan.

She reached up and moved his hair away from a bloody cut, but he made no move to her gentle touch. Above Braz, his door window glass was gone and white flakes lazily drifted in; his dark sweater was already covered with a layer of white, while snow crystals meandered down and melted on Katelyn's face.

Katelyn tried to push herself off the inside of the door, now the bottom of her world, but couldn't lift herself enough to get out of the water. She didn't know if her feet were just too numb or if they were lodged under a portion of the dashboard. Reaching behind she got a grip on the seat headrest and managed to move her body a couple of inches enough to bend her stiffening knees. She kept inching her soaked legs towards her until she could see her boots. The light was sufficient in the grey gloom of the cab for Katelyn to see that her feet appeared uninjured.

Desperation caused her to twist her head around, looking for answers. The front windshield was still intact and Katelyn could see a water line lapping on the outside of the glass. The water level inside the truck underneath her was almost at the same height as outside.

"Well, I won't drown," she said out loud to bolster her courage. "But hypothermia is not too far off," her teeth chattered.

She was starting to lose all feeling in her legs driving her to focus on only one thought: get out of the water. She looked up and saw that she could possibly reach the tube supporting the driver's headrest behind her father. Stretching out she inched her left hand up to the headrest and could just grasp the support tube with several fingers.

"Move, Katelyn!" she yelled out loud.

With a lunge of her remaining strength, she pulled herself up enough to prop herself on the driver-side bucket seat while curled up over and behind her father, her body wedged between his back and seat. Her feet were still in the water and completely numb but her legs and upper body were now free of the frigid stream. She took a moment to rest her head on the driver seatbelt. Relief flooded her thoughts at her successful climb, but more so because she felt her father's strong breathing.

Lethargy, however, began spreading its dangerous tendrils through her body and mind. As Katelyn's thinking began to cloud, she shook her head. She couldn't frame any words to pray, so she just breathed a sigh of help to the heavens. And then a voice like a thousand crystal bells rang in her mind, jolting her fully awake.

The voice was melody and sang in her heart of its love for her over and over. Its sound woke an intense longing so strong that it felt like every cell in her clamored to run into its embrace. Words of endearment flashed across her mind in a steady stream: *precious friend*, *beloved*. She tried to capture them, focus upon their joy, but they flew out of reach to be replaced with something lovelier, deeper, and more alive. As she relaxed in the flow of love the language began changing. She caught affection in phrases of French and Italian but they too flew into the maelstrom of her feelings, until the languages became a murmuring of angels that human tongues had never framed.

Desire pulsed in every vein. She wanted. She needed. She yearned for the embrace that was offered in every breath, and that grew in splendor with every heartbeat. An awareness bloomed within her that she could take all that was revealed, what she sensed beyond her greatest imaginings, and still never exhaust its bounty. And with every grasping of proffered life, joy rebounded. Her taking was met with laughter and light as the song reveled in her receiving.

With the song came a strange harmony of mixed notes. It not only blended with the giving and receiving of love but wound its way down to the depths of her soul. As the main song continued to breathe its joy to Katelyn's mind the harmony reached to where a door was locked and gently wooed it to open. She heard a voice behind the door scream in terror, but the harmony did not relent.

She heard the harmony speak to the door. "I will never leave you. I will always be with you."

The voice screamed from the other side. "You left me. You left me. You promised me. You left me!"

An image suddenly came into her mind, as clear as if it was yesterday. Her mom was holding her hand while lying in the hospital bed. Katelyn still remembered the feel of her mother's dry skin, the boniness of her fingers and the weak grip. Her mother was whispering with closed eyes, "I will always be with you, little one. Do not be afraid."

Katelyn remembered sobbing as her mother's hand relaxed and she breathed her last.

And then Katelyn was at the ceiling of the room, looking down at herself holding her mother's hand, a perspective beyond any memory. The scene took on an unusual brightness. She heard the same song and melody of love still washing over her in the truck, but this time saw the Singer. He was almost too bright to behold; the same song of love enveloping her mother in waves of rainbow colors. He held her other hand, and heard him singing over and over again to her mother, "I will always be with you, little one. Do not be afraid."

As the scene continued, Katelyn witnessed a tendril of blackness inking its way into the room and flowing toward her as she held her mother's hand. She watched, both from the ceiling, and reliving the emotions of the moment, the blackness blossoming into a cloud around her mind.

With a strange insight, Katelyn realized that her mother was mouthing the words being sung to her from the Singer, and not giving Katelyn a final blessing.

She saw herself holding her mother's hand, with no sight of the encroaching darkness. The pain of her loss etched on her face, as she was somehow able to watch her mother's words, entwined with the twisted smoke, barreling deep into her heart, carrying with it a vow: everyone will abandon you; you are not worthy to be loved.

At that moment the Singer raised his eyes and looked at Katelyn floating near the ceiling. Katelyn became lost in the depths of his passion. As he smiled at her, his joy flowed into the room, erasing the darkness surrounding her sobbing form, as if it never was.

The Singer turned to grasp her mother's hand but not before he uttered a simple statement to Katelyn that shattered the lie she had been holding onto for years.

You are worthy to be loved.

The scene in her mind abruptly shut off and only the faint sounds of the falling snow returned her to focus on her plight in the truck. Katelyn breathed deeply with closed eyes, realizing with wonder that something crusted over her soul was gone.

And then a wave of pressure pounded through her veins. Her body felt infused with strength, as if she could soar from the confines of the truck and hurl it into the sky. She shifted her stance to completely pull her feet out of the water and moved to stand in the back seat, behind her father. Warmth flowed from the deepest recesses of her heart into her arms, legs, and toes. Energy flickered at the end of her fingertips and then leaped from her hand into her father, infusing him likewise with strength. And as she released love into his unconscious body, she felt it stir with new life. She sensed a sweetness beyond any sensation, from the simple act of giving.

Braz stirred but Katlyn's attention was still focused on the music. It began to quiet and the tingling of every nerve in her body calmed. A gentle voice filled her mind, whispering a question into the sudden stillness. *What do you want, Katelyn?*

The question lingered in the air while she caught the expectant whisperings of countless voices waiting for her answer, as if the entire world could not move forward without her reply. There was only one answer that came unbidden into her thoughts; one request after tasting a goodness beyond life, of glimpsing of a well of love that could never run dry. Only one thing could be asked after feeling the immensity of a tender heart that had given its very being in ransom for her, and set her free from the blackness of her bondage.

"Just to thank you," Katelyn spoke within. She closed her eyes to the calmest peace surrounding her while the music in her heart swelled into a cacophony of praise. As she breathed out a smile, she felt a sudden tuft of fresh snowflakes fall onto her face. She opened her eyes to see Ethan peering down at her from just a few inches away. He was breathing heavy, and his normal weird grin was replaced instead with a stricken expression.

"Katelyn!" was all he could shout at seeing her face. He looked like he was ready to tear the door off the truck.

"Ethan," too, was all she could reply. She reached up and lightly placed her hand on his cheek. "I'm good – I'm not hurt."

Katelyn could see Ethan's fear evaporating with her touch. Within seconds he was joined at the broken window opening by the anguished faces of Natalie and Ben.

"Kat, are you...?" Natalie gasped.

"Yes, I'm fine – actually more than fine. We need to help Dad."

Katelyn inched backwards and propped herself up against the back seat and window. The back seat already contained several inches of snow that had fallen in from the broken side windows. None of the doors would open, and Katelyn found her father's seatbelt release button jammed, so the boys worked at cutting Braz loose through the driver window frame with a pocket knife. Braz shook his head awake in alarm as they were half finished.

"Where is Katelyn?" he asked in panic.

"Back here Dad," she answered, putting a hand on his shoulder. "I'm fine – really. And don't rebuke Ben and Ethan for working on you first. Once you are out, I can crawl through your window opening."

"Alright," he mumbled. "Work faster, boys."

They finally sawed through the tough seatbelt and helped guide Braz out of the window and then down into the river. They had been standing in the snow and slush up to their calves, and Braz plopped into the freezing stream without a complaint. All three men helped guide Katelyn out of the window opening as she climbed into Ben's arms. Natalie walked arm in arm with Braz while Ethan helped stabilize Ben, as the group trudged around the truck and out of the stream of frozen slush and snow.

As Ben started struggling up the steep embankment Katelyn said, "Ben – put me down. I can walk without a problem. I feel great, and you are more liable to fall and have us both roll into the water."

Ben reluctantly set Katelyn gently down. She quickly clambered up the muddy and icy hillside first, arriving at the top with an energetic leap. Janet and several of the youth advisors, along with Josiah, were there to meet them at the roadside, with panic-stricken looks that quickly changed to awe. Braz slowly followed Katelyn up the snow-trampled hill, and then everyone mobbed the two as Janet tried to check them for major cuts or broken bones.

"We're good, but so glad to see all of you," Katelyn cried. Everyone started hugging through their tears.

Ethan stood at the outskirts of the group enjoying the reunion as his grin returned. He asked Josiah to wait as he headed back to the pickup for stuff left behind, while Janet bundled Katelyn and Braz into her warm truck. Ben and Natalie climbed in with them.

"You both do look fine but do you want me to take you to a hospital?" she asked as she passed out several blankets. "With this weather, we can be there in about an hour."

"I don't feel sore at all," Braz said. "I actually feel quite invigorated." He looked at Katelyn curiously.

"I'm great, Janet. No, just take us back," Katelyn spoke. Janet stared at them for several seconds before putting the truck in gear. She backed around on the snow-covered road, and then slowly drove towards to the ranch, several miles away. The other adults and college students who had driven up also headed back, while Josiah and Kara waited for Ethan in Josiah's compact Subaru.

Katelyn sat in the back, with Braz and Natalie on either side giving her a detailed inspection regardless of her continued reassurances that she was fine. Ben turned around from the front seat and likewise looked over Katelyn with concern. She grabbed a hand from both sides and announced, "Please don't worry. I, we, were miraculously protected, and I don't feel pain anywhere. No," she responded to Janet's eyes in the rear-view mirror, "I am not in shock."

Janet smiled back in the mirror and just nodded.

"But I would like to know how you all came to our rescue so fast?"

Ben answered soberly, "It was all Janet's idea. Somehow, she was convinced that something had happened to you. When neither of you answered your cell phones, Janet headed out to find you. Several cars followed us, and again it was Janet who first spotted the overturned truck in the river. But Katelyn – we weren't fast at all. From the snow covering the truck's sides, it looked like you had been in the water for at least an hour. So, can you tell us why you and your father are not dead from the cold, and how come all your clothes are practically dry? Just a couple of minutes in that water and my feet are practically numb, but you look...well, like you just got back from shopping."

Katelyn reached for her phone, which was no longer in her pocket, while Braz glanced at his watch. Braz spoke with surprise, "It *has* been about sixty minutes since we crashed. I have no recollection after being knocked out, I think from hitting Katelyn's head." Braz reached up to feel the side of his head where dried blood made a dark contrast against his thick silver hair but could not find a wound or bump.

Katelyn moved slightly to glance at her own head in Janet's rear view mirror, and likewise could not see any swelling or colored skin where she was sure she had slammed into something hard. As she felt her clothes the memories of the crash flooded her emotions. Tears quickly began falling down Katelyn's cheek and she raised a hand to Ben's sudden intense look of concern.

Katelyn whispered in awe, "I *was* dying. I had been lying in the freezing water and was soaked through. The parts of my body that were not numb or turning blue ached with pain from multiple bruises. I managed to prop myself over dad's seat, then...," she paused. Catching Janet's eye in the rear-view mirror she continued, "I was immersed in music."

Katelyn brushed tears from her eyes, and said to Janet's reflection in the mirror, "You know what I heard, don't you?"

Janet's reply was simply, "Here – we're back. If you change your mind and want to go to the hospital, just find me or call me and I'll get you there faster than any ambulance can arrive. I am so glad that neither of you are hurt. And Katelyn, after you rest up come tell me the details of what happened at the Double Bar D. I talked to Franz after you left there and he called you an angel. Great job."

Janet got out of her truck and went inside the office, while Ben, Natalie, Braz, and Katelyn sloshed into the lodge. They all headed to their rooms to change and clean up, but not before being met with hugs and exclamations of joy by their friends waiting in the foyer. Begging off any questions, Katelyn promised to share about their ordeal at the service that evening. Ben and Natalie did not let her off as easily as they walked up the steps to their rooms, trailing Braz's wet footprints.

"I want the whole story, Kat," Natalie said.

"And I don't want the Cliff Notes version at the service tonight," Ben chimed in.

"Fine," Katelyn said. "Looks like we have some time before dinner. How about we meet in the little sitting area with the comfy chairs at the end of our hallway? We should be alone."

"OK," Ben said. "I'll sneak up but you have to come to my aid if any of the chaperones catch me on the girls' floor. Because I want to hear this. Really. Something's happened to you and I'm intrigued."

Katelyn laughed. "Sure Ben, but I have something more for you than a story." She pushed him down his hallway as he gave her a questioning look. As the two girls climbed the remaining steps to their floor Natalie tried to get some advanced news, but Katelyn just shook her head and said, "Wait, Nat – it will be worth it."

Katelyn took one last look back down into the dining room but didn't see the one she truly wanted to share with.

16. Gifts

Ethan climbed into the back of Josiah's car with Katelyn's purse, cell phone, keys, and some important water-soaked papers. He was silent and Josiah and Kara did not interrupt his thoughts for most of the ride back. Finally, Josiah asked, "How did they survive that accident without even a scratch, Ethan?"

"I don't know," he said. "Multiple rollovers. The inside looks like a war zone with glass everywhere."

"It must have been angels," Kara said in awe, to which Josiah snorted, and Kara glared back.

"I'm sure Katelyn will give some explanation, later," Ethan said. He knew something wonderful had happened but was content to wait. He had never seen anything more beautiful than her shining face, dotted with snowflakes, peering out of the broken window – alive and apparently unhurt. He leaned back and closed his eyes wanting to just replay that scene over in his mind when a familiar nudge inside him interrupted his thoughts.

Really? Now? Frustration bubbled up. Haven't we had enough opportunities this weekend?

The voice inside him chuckled and then whispered to him, *There will be much more time ahead to focus on Katelyn. I need you to give Josiah and Kara a gift.*

Ethan sighed and cracked open his eyes. One quick glance at Kara and Josiah was enough to confirm the tension between them. He considered some gentle opening discussion but irritation drove him to a more direct confrontation.

Ethan spoke to Kara first. "Kara, do you love Josiah?" He could see the blush on Kara's face from the back seat.

"Ethan, I -" Kara started, but Ethan interrupted with the same question. Anger now sparked in Kara's backward glance, but Ethan did not relent and asked a third time, "Kara, do you love that man beside you?"

She turned towards Josiah, and quietly whispered, "Yes."

Before she could continue with a "but" Ethan knew was coming, he asked Josiah, "Josiah do you love Kara?"

Josiah looked back at Ethan in the mirror with a pained expression but didn't answer. Ethan said, "Josiah, do you want me to keep asking you?" Kara was now focused intently upon Josiah, with a look that could boil steel.

Ethan waited and Josiah finally said without taking his gaze away from the road in front of him, "No – you do not have to ask again. The answer is of course, yes," he said, glancing back at Ethan again through the mirror.

"I only have one more question for you Josiah," Ethan said, finally warming to the opportunity. "Why are you telling *me* this?"

Josiah's grip on the steering wheel tightened and then without taking his eyes off the road, he stepped on the brake and slowly brought the car to a stop. When the car was fully stopped, he shifted into "Park" and then turned to the fiery little redhead next to him.

"Kara, I love you," Josiah said softly with longing and sadness. "I'm sorry for how I spoke to you at the studio."

Kara's eyes flashed and then she was unbuckling her seat belt and lunging over the stick shift to hug and kiss Josiah. Apologies followed more hugs and kisses and Ethan was momentarily forgotten. After a few minutes, Ethan cleared his throat and the two lovers in front stopped, though to Ethan neither looked embarrassed.

Josiah and Kara still hadn't taken their eyes off each other when Ethan spoke, "OK – one more time…" Ethan couldn't hear the very quiet words shared but could catch some of the "I love you" words framed by their lips, and he was forgotten again.

After a minute Ethan laughed and said, "My feet and legs are almost frozen back here!"

As Kara and Josiah reluctantly separated and Josiah put the car in gear Ethan spoke to the familiar one inside of him. I must admit, that was cool. Thanks. I hope I remember this lesson in the future.

Ethan could sense a satisfied smile. Love whispered to his heart again, *That was a little more direct than I would have approached it, but well done. Don't worry, I'll remind you of this lesson. And – you will need to be reminded, often. Now you can go back to meditating on Katelyn's beauty.*

And then the voice was quiet, though Ethan could sense a bridled joy.

When Josiah arrived at the main lodge and parked, Ethan whipped out of the car with a quick acknowledgment to both Josiah's and Kara's thankyou nods and tromped into the building. There was a festive air in the entire foyer. He glanced towards the fireplace and heard giggling and laughing from several of the youth. Braz had already returned with a change of clothes and was regaling several of the adult advisors in another corner about the funny ranch hands at the Double Bar D. As he walked to the dining room, he caught the advisors who had confronted Janet earlier talking to her and thanking her for her sensitivity in arousing everyone to go search for Braz and Katelyn. They even asked if they could come watch her dance sometimes. Loud singing of "Be Our Guest" from *Beauty and the Beast* was coming from the kitchen workers as Ethan headed up the stairs, and several raucous groups were playing games at the dining room tables.

Ethan ran up to his room, grabbed some fresh clothes and headed for the showers. He avoided anything that looked like it might be homemade shampoo and cleaned up. Back in his room he put on two pairs of socks, his feet still cold, and then scrunched on his dry running shoes. Grabbing Katelyn's stuff, Ethan went out in the hallway and waited at the stairs, hoping to catch a girl heading up to the women's floor for a hand-off.

Ethan was about to give up when a strong hand grabbed his elbow from behind and started dragging him along up the steps. Before Ethan could object Ben said quietly, "Come on buddy – we've been invited, but be quiet. If Mrs. 'I'll have your hide if I see any male above the second floor' sees us we are toast. I might have to join the military," he smiled.

They both quietly walked down the hall listening for possible opening doors and hugging the walls when the dining room appeared through the handrails. They reached the end of the women's hallway without incident, however, and seated themselves in wingback chairs in a wide hidden nook; their seats hidden from the hallway. The area was lit with the after-storm sunshine blazing through a small, curtained window.

"That was fun. Sneaking should prepare you well for West Point," Ethan said. "Can you tell me what's going on?" he quietly asked.

"Katelyn is coming with Natalie and is going to share what happened in the truck."

Ethan suddenly got nervous. "Did Katelyn really ask me here?"

"No, but I'm sure if you were with us when we were talking, she would have. She would want to share this with you."

Ethan stood up and said, "Thanks. I appreciate the consideration. I really do. But, for some reason I can't explain, I have the strongest sensation I need to leave. I shouldn't be here, though I would love to stay and listen."

"What? You getting some vibes that the chaperone is around the corner?"

"No." Ethan handed Katelyn's things to Ben, and said, "I have to go – now." Without waiting for Ben to reply, Ethan rushed down the hallway, then down the stairs to the dining room.

"That's a strange guy," Ben remarked out loud, trying to figure out what just happened.

"Who is strange?" Natalie said quietly, coming around the corner with Katelyn.

"Ah, nobody."

Katelyn saw her purse and phone in Ben's hands. "Ethan! Was he just here?"

"Yeah, he couldn't stay. So, what is this gift you have for me?" Ben asked. "And tell us all about the angels with hair dryers everybody is speculating about."

Katelyn glanced back down the hallway, saddened that Ethan had left without a word. But she turned back and the joy of her encounter in the truck soon eclipsed her disappointment. She took a chair and moved it between Ben and Natalie.

Glancing to either side, she said, "Well, where to start? First – no angels I can remember. Ok. How about I start when we turned off the highway and my dad was asking me for permission to let him start dating again."

Katelyn then replayed her encounter to the amazement of her friends. "And then Ethan and you guys showed up," she finished.

Both Ben and Natalie were speechless and sat there in the fading afternoon light with various emotions playing across their faces.

"Kat, that was wonderful," Natalie said. "Somehow, I felt like I was in the truck with you as you shared."

"Thanks," Ben echoed. "That was...amazing."

Katelyn scooted her chair closer to her friends and took a hand from each of them in hers. Natalie's eyes grew wide, while Ben sat there with a curious expression on his face. "It *was* an amazing experience. I felt like I have been given a special gift, though it may take me some time to fully understand it. But I have something else to share," Katelyn said with a growing excitement.

She first looked at Ben with sparkling eyes and then to Natalie with a slightly mischievous grin. "I need to apologize, to both of you."

She paused, took a deep breath and continued. "I walled off my heart, my feelings, and my love for both of you after mom died. You were there the whole time, supporting me but I pushed you away."

Katelyn shifted her glance back and forth between Natalie and Ben, and said, "I became blind to each of your hearts. I covered my eyes and my ears to how you tried to lift me up, and in doing so failed to see the lie actually drawing me deeper into the very fear I imagined."

She smiled to the heavens and whispered, "A lie cannot stand the truth. One only needs to turn on the light."

"I promise to try harder and listen to every ounce of love you have for me from now on. But we have changed – all of us. We need a new road. And the path down that road starts with a promise."

With hands still clasped, Katelyn stood, bringing up Ben and Natalie closer to her.

"No – Kat," Natalie breathed. She wormed her hand out of Katelyn's grasp and covered her mouth.

Without letting go of Ben, Katelyn laughed and the melody of bells she heard in the truck filled her heart. She reached up to Natalie's face and slowly pried her fist away from her mouth, holding it gently, once again. Katelyn's face had such delight that Natalie finally calmed and relaxed the tension in her grip. Natalie then looked up through moist eyes at Ben with an expectant hope. Katelyn turned back to Ben, a master strategist, who looked clueless.

She released her clasp with her friends' hands and put Natalie's hand in Ben's. She then said to both of them, "Let love prosper."

Ben glanced down at Natalie's hand, and then to the smiling face of Katelyn. His eyes widened in awe as he glanced back and forth between Natalie and Katelyn. Katelyn gave Ben a slight nod, who shyly looked down again at Natalie's small soft hand enfolded in his own. He looked up and watched a joyous grin blossom on Natalie's face as a single tear squeezed from each eye.

Ben reached up with his free hand and caught each tear before it fell from Natalie's face then grasped her other hand. Katelyn stepped back as Ben and Natalie unconsciously moved a step closer.

As they got lost in each other's sight Katelyn silently left the alcove, wrapped in the joy of heaven.

17. Goodbyes

Katelyn walked carefully up the slick, snow-covered trail, peering through the misty beginning of Sunday morning. The upward path turned a corner about twenty yards ahead. The automatic lamp posts along the way tripped off as she hiked up the sodden and snow-filled bark footpath, giving her the feeling that the whole forest was beckoning her on. Turning the bend, she saw Ethan a little further up the path, sitting atop the huge boulder where the trail split. Stopping in front of the rock she looked up at him, his legs dangling about two feet above her head.

"Is there room for two?" she asked.

"Absolutely," Ethan answered, patting the stone. "There is a path up the side over there," he motioned. "It's a sharp climb but follow my boot prints in the snow."

Katelyn slowly made her way around the granite remnant from some long-gone glacier. Ethan leaned over the edge to lend her a hand as she traversed the steep slope, then helped her step out onto the top. There was a thick wool blanket covering the surprisingly flat surface.

"The blanket is a nice touch. I didn't fancy sitting on a cold, wet rock," she said.

"Janet told you I had something to show you?" Ethan asked.

"I was looking for you before we took off for home, and when I asked Janet where you were, she just told me you were waiting for me here. She called it the prayer rock. Couldn't you have picked a cozier spot in front of the fire?"

"It *is* a perfect place for praying, and I have had some amazing conversations up here. But today it is not about speaking – just receiving."

The word "receiving" reminded Katelyn of music so she relaxed and leaned against Ethan's side.

Ethan pointed through their frozen breaths in the crisp, cold air straight ahead towards the east. About fifty yards away was a large gap in the snow-covered pine trees that ringed the main lodge, way below them. The massive Rocky Mountain range displayed their grandeur through the opening. Though miles away, sharp crags and multiple peaks were visible, jutting up from huge forests. All was generally gray but the early morning light was beginning to reveal the glistening caps of white from the recent snowfall.

As Katelyn watched, a sliver of the sun appeared at the left edge of the opening, peeking above the mountain range. Remnants of the dark storm clouds began turning into a patchwork of brilliant orange and lavender hues as the bright orb revealed itself. Holding their breaths, they watched as the far mountains began sparkling with brilliant colors and the white forest in front of them transformed into an artist's palette. The sun finally disappeared into the higher scattered storm clouds but not before it had bathed the boulder in a shaft of brilliant yellow light.

"That was gorgeous," Katelyn remarked in awe.

Ethan said, "Not as beautiful as the one sitting beside me, but majestic nonetheless." Katelyn smiled and leaned closer against Ethan, resting her head upon his shoulder.

"The story that you shared last night of your encounter in the crash was amazing," Ethan said. "I got the feeling looking around that it was inspiring all kinds of sentiments in the group, especially with your two best friends," he said amusingly.

"It was nothing less than the inspiration you gave a certain youth pastor and his fiancé," Katelyn replied with a sardonic smile.

Ethan chuckled and moved his arm around her shoulders.

"So, Dad is going to cover the difference from your insurance on a new truck?"

"Only after I threatened to get a good lawyer and sue him," Ethan laughed. He sniffed the air around Katelyn's shiny hair. "Frankincense and myrrh?"

Katelyn didn't answer but smiled in the sunlight, reappearing through the broken clouds.

"I was thinking," he said, keeping his eyes on the distant mountains. "Though I am near to graduating, I am going to change my major from business. I had a short conversation with your father this morning and I am going to study law. With my current credits, it shouldn't take too long to earn a degree majoring in pre-law."

Katelyn pulled away from Ethan in surprise and stared up at him. Ethan asked, "You don't think I would make a good lawyer?"

"Well sure, I guess," she stumbled.

"Thanks for the vote of confidence,' he smiled. "I hear there is a great pre-law program at the University of Washington, and I would still be close enough to help out my aunt."

Katelyn broke Ethan's gaze and straightened, staring out through the drooping cedar branches. "Yes, their program is one of the best in the nation," she said with an edge of sadness. She emptily watched clumps of snow drop from the upper boughs of the pine trees to land silently in the snow drifts below.

"What?" Ethan softly breathed into her hair.

Katelyn took a moment and then answered, "We haven't talked yet but I had hoped that..."

She stopped as the emotions swirling in her heart rose up and clenched her throat.

Ethan remained silent for several moments, and as Katelyn didn't seem able to finish her sentence, he continued.

"Speaking of best in the nation, did you know that Cornell University, in New York, is one of the top-rated veterinarian schools in the country?"

Without waiting for an answer, he said, "You may not know it, but Janet attended there in their vet program for several years."

"Yes, Janet shared that with me last night," Katelyn vacantly spoke into the air, still trying to piece together her own thoughts from Ethan's new plans. "She was really supportive of me going there. It looks like an awesome program," she finished, trying to keep the sadness out of her voice.

"Well, Janet told me this morning that she had sent one of the professors she knows there an email to scope out a slot in their program for you, and that he had already positively replied. It looks like a fantastic opportunity. And when Ben gets into West Point next year, I hear that Natalie will transfer to the chemistry program at Rensselaer Polytechnic in Troy, New York. You will all only be a couple of hours away from each other."

Katelyn's curiosity at how Ethan knew about Natalie's plans was overwhelmed by a growing emotion. "Yes." Katelyn whispered, not trusting her voice to remain steady.

"I have every confidence that you will do great there," Ethan continued. "Of course, veterinarian training is a very long program…"

As Ethan paused, Katelyn thought about what had really been gained this weekend. While the prospect of attending a top-notch veterinary school promised to be a wonderful step for her future, and the physical closeness of her two friends another amazing opportunity, it all felt hollow against being separated from the growing friendship of this man at her side.

The dreams that had begun to bud over the last several days threatened to whither, and all the tomorrows with Ethan started blurring into mist. Fears clamored for her attention. She felt as if she were being pulled back to her mother's hospital bed.

Before the knot in Katelyn's throat rose to shatter her remaining hopes, her eye caught a shaft of light brightening the nearby Ponderosa fir. The sun caused the snow on the branches to sparkle and glimpses of emerald appeared where the light painted its brightness on the underlying branches. The glistening color reminded Katelyn of a riddle on a snowy night. As understanding blossomed, the fear and pain retreated.

A far green country isn't something in the future, she thought. It is not even something one needs to search for long and hard. It is never more than a heartbeat away.

Thankfulness flooded her heart, and she prayed silently. Thank you for the amazing miracles and healing you have done this weekend. Thank you especially for helping me see that you have never given up on me; you have always been here, experiencing my doubt and pain with me. I can hardly see any of the future with Ethan but I am going to trust that you have more planned than just these last several days, even more than the few remaining months till we head our separate ways. Thanks for helping me start to believe, again.

Katelyn stopped as the sound of bells and music flooded her mind again, with a yearning so strong that she could not breathe.

Katelyn, she heard reverberate in her mind with notes of elation. *I want so much more than your belief*!

She unconsciously stiffened and wondered if all the fragile pieces of her faith that were beginning to mend might fly apart. The voice sang even louder in her mind, drowning out the feelings of inadequacy and shame, that threatened once again to drive her into blackness. It ended in stillness with a question she thought she would never hear again.

Katelyn, what do you want?

Her fear ebbed away as she set her thoughts to one more mystery. Ethan's final words that strange evening replayed in her mind: a far green country is a land where there is no shame in desire, but more than just a place. Then, the light that had dawned in the studio after dancing blossomed again into understanding.

She gasped. She knew then what she wanted, what she had always wanted. And she now knew the source. And as the words came unbidden to her mind, she realized with awe that her need was birthed from the amazing one within her, and his desire.

She relaxed her grip on Ethan's arm. A far green country is an indwelling of love – His presence!

While the distant peaks again became bathed with ochre and vermillion hues, Katelyn softly answered deep in her spirit something that she had buried a long time ago: to embrace your presence.

A door opened deep within her, and this time was met not with a screaming voice but instead with a voice singing, *Come my beloved*!

Katelyn then echoed that same phrase with a pleasure that filled every vacant hope. It repeated in her mind, as a rapturous melody, again and again, until she could not tell whose voice was singing.

The singing ebbed, and as Katelyn's eyes refocused on the world of snow, trees, and sunshine, she felt Ethan tremble. A window opened in her mind and she was able to catch that same voice of love within her speaking to Ethan from a similar depth.

Now! it said.

With a giddy voice, Ethan finished his sentence, "And New York is *way* on the other side of the country from Seattle."

Katelyn blinked. Somehow, she felt more than heard the grin on Ethan's face. She took her chilled hands out of her pocket, reached up, and gently turned Ethan's face down towards her. With an expectation twinkling in moist eyes she asked, "What are we discussing here, Ethan McGregor?"

"Do you think your father will object to us sharing an apartment in New York?" Ethan asked. "After all," he drolly continued, "you have already slept in my bed."

"Ethan…" Katelyn breathed.

Ethan's reddened cheeks stretched wide to contain his beaming face. "I just applied online this morning to Cornell's pre-law program – Dr. Katelyn Braselli, Cornell veterinarian," Ethan said.

Katelyn dropped her hands and punched his arm with all her might.

"Of course, he would object! And, did you think to ask me first?" she said, her voice rising over Ethan's mock exclamation of pain. "I object, too!" she shouted.

Ethan's eyes dove into Katelyn's tear-filled gaze as he said, "It was only the smallest of faith that kept me imagining you were not lost to me, dearest Katelyn. And now that I have found you, I will follow you anywhere. I will never stop following you." He then gently took her face in his hands and kissed her with the hunger of waiting years.

Small snowflakes drifted in the morning air and landed on Katelyn and Ethan as they embraced in the brightening day. Ethan pulled back to gaze into eyes that were filled with the sun. Their kiss resumed as Katelyn responded with a longing that now sang in crashing waves. They finally separated but only by a couple of inches. Katelyn gave Ethan a playful smile, as both faces reflected their unconfined joy.

"It will probably be alright to visit me, though," she said, trailing a hand through his hair and over his face. "I might even let you take me out on a date. We will just have to wait and see."

Ethan smiled back in delight. "Have I told you how lovely you look in the morning?"

"Not recently," she breathed against his lips. "You better keep practicing."

The End

Author Bio

A.R. "Rick" Tedeschi is passionate about Jesus' presence in our lives. More than just a metaphor, Rick believes in the immeasurable promise that Christ can live inside a person. It is his joy to share the wonders of the Holy Spirit's life indwelling a believer and fascination to explore the riddles of our heavenly Father's presence expressed within. This relationship of Jesus living in us is the ultimate romance, and is witnessed in the stories of all our relationships. As a husband, father, grandfather, friend, engineer, manager, project manager, and most importantly a child of God, relationships are the center of his life, and it is his prayer that his stories would help deepen all of yours. Rick lives in southeastern Washington surrounded by many precious family and friends.

Check out more on his website "An Indwelling Presence" at https://www.ricktedeschi.com/. God bless you!